Puffin Books

This Little Puffin . . .

This remarkable treasury of finger plays and
singing and action games will be a delight and
a blessing for anyone who wishes to persuade
young children to join in musical activities,
either in groups or individually.

Each of the rhymes, songs and singing games has
been well tried and proved popular since this
working collection was compiled with the help
of nursery school teachers all over the country
by Elizabeth Matterson – ex-Chairman of the
National Association of Pre-School Playgroups
and a Course Tutor to nursery nurses – and
author of the very useful Penguin Handbook
Play with a Purpose for Under-Sevens.

This Little Puffin...

Finger Plays and Nursery Games
compiled by
Elizabeth Matterson

Chapter headings by *Raymond Briggs*
Other decorations by *David Woodroffe*

Puffin Books

Puffin Books, Penguin Books Ltd, Harmondsworth, Middlesex, England
Penguin Books, 625 Madison Avenue, New York, New York 10022, U.S.A.
Penguin Books Australia Ltd, Ringwood, Victoria, Australia
Penguin Books Canada Ltd, 2801 John Street, Markham, Ontario, Canada L3R 1B4
Penguin Books (N.Z.) Ltd, 182–190 Wairau Road, Auckland 10, New Zealand

Published in Puffin Books 1969
Reprinted 1970 (twice), 1971 (twice), 1972, 1973 (twice),
1974, 1975 (twice), 1976, 1977, 1978, 1979 (twice), 1980, 1981 (twice), 1982, 1983

Made and printed in Great Britain by
Hazell Watson & Viney Ltd, Aylesbury, Bucks
Set in Monotype Bembo

TIP ME UP
AND POUR ME
OUT

Contents

Acknowledgements

The editor and publishers gratefully acknowledge the permission of the following to include copyright poems in this book:

W. Paxton & Co. Ltd for *Oh, what shall we do in our garden*, from *More Singing Games* by Edith Kay, *To and fro*, from *Little Songs with Rhythmic Movement* by Jennifer Day, *Slowly, slowly walks my Grandad*, from *Playway to Rhythmics* by A. W. I. Chitty, *Pretty little pussycat*, from *Five for Fun* by Marion Anderson, *Can you walk on two legs* and *Fingers Like to Wiggle Waggle*, from *Play Songs for the Nursery School* by Lindford Holgate, *Mr Lynn is very thin*, from *Finger Play Fun* by A. W. I. Chitty, *See my fingers walking* and *Down in the grass, curled up in a heap*, from *Finger Play Songs* by A. W. I. Chitty, *How does a caterpillar go*, *If you were a beech tree*, and *See each India rubber ball*, from *Physical Training Action Songs* by M. C. Dainton; Mills Music Ltd for *When all the cows were sleeping*, from *Wide Awake* by M. Russell-Smith and G. Russell-Smith; James Nisbet and Company Ltd for *Sometimes I'm very, very small*, by Ethel Hedley from *Rhymes and Dances for Little Folk* by Celia Sparger; George G. Harrap and Company Ltd for *What does the clock in the hall say*, *Aeroplanes, aeroplanes all in a row*, *Jump, jump Kangaroo Brown*, *Puffer train, puffer train*, *Five little sparrows*, *See the little bunny sleeping*, and *Heads and shoulders, knees and toes*, from *Music for the Nursery School* by Linda Chesterman; J. Curwen and Sons Ltd for *Mother's washing* and *With my little broom I sweep, sweep, sweep* from *New Nursery Jingles* by E. Barnard, *I can knock with my two hands* and *Up I stretch on tippy toe* from *Nursery School Music Activities* by E. Barnard, *There's a little ball* by Louie de Rusette, from *Three, Four, Five*; *Here is a beehive*, and *Here's a ball for baby* by Emilie Poulson; Stainer and Bell Ltd for *Help me wind my ball of wool*, *Pray open your umbrella*, *Tall shop in the town*, *The elephant is big and strong*, *Long legs, long legs slowly stalking*, *I have made a pretty nest*, and *Little Arabella Miller*, from *Fingers and Thumbs* by Ann Elliott, also *Here Comes a Policeman* by E. Barnard from *Echo and Refrain Songs* © 1939; J. B. Cramer and Company Ltd for *A tall thin man, walking along*, and *I love to row in my big blue boat* from *Playtime Tunes for the Nursery School* by Marion Anderson; Sir Isaac Pitman and Sons Ltd for *A mouse lived in a little hole*, *I had a little cherry stone*, *Here is the ostrich straight and tall*, and *Here is a tree with its leaves so green*, from *Nursery Rhymes and Finger Plays* by Boyce and Bartlett; Evans Brothers Ltd for *This is the way we wash our clothes* and *My Wellington boots*, by Lilian

McCrea, *There's such a tiny little mouse* by Thurza Wakely, *Four scarlet berries* by Mary Vivian, and *The policeman walks with heavy tread* by E. M. Adams, all from *The Book of a Thousand Poems*, Miss M. J. Chaplin for *Here is a house with two little people*, Mrs Wyn Daniel Evans for *A tiny, tiny worm, Five Little Ducks, One, Two, Three, Four* and *Ten Galloping Horses*, Mrs Jean Chadwick for *Three Jelly Fish*, and Faber Music Ltd (on behalf of J. Curwen & Sons Ltd) for *Three Little Pigs* by Anne Mendoza from *Seven Simple Songs for Children*.

Thanks are also due to the many nursery school teachers who not only sent lists of the songs they use but also copied out the music and rhymes in those cases where they could not be traced. In addition, three people most generously allowed their own original work to be included: Mrs G. Moore of Worksop, Notts., who wrote *Mummy has scissors* and *Softly, softly, falling so*; Mrs J. E. Riley of Bradford, Yorkshire, who wrote *Let's see the monkeys*; and Miss Catherine Willis of Atherstone, Warwickshire, who wrote *Raise your hands above your head* and *If I were a little bird*.

Introduction

There are many excellent reasons for using music and rhymes with young children. Children learn to speak by imitating, they develop voice control by repeating rhymes and songs. Action songs provide exercise and encourage body control, the more energetic songs offer an opportunity to use thwarted energy on wet days. Ring games help social development when everyone has to take his turn and play his part. Every mother knows how songs soothe a fractious baby, while away a wearisome car journey or distract a frightened child. But the best reason for singing and acting together is that it is fun. At home it offers valuable contact between adult and children and most families develop their own repertoire of bed-time and 'silly' time songs. At Nursery School or Playgroup, music sessions are the time when everyone does the same thing at the same time.

This collection of songs and activities has been made by asking Nursery School teachers what their children like best. The very large list resulting from this has included some very old songs and some very new ones, showing regional favourites and many variations. In most cases the teachers had no idea where the songs originated but had learned and developed their repertoire in the manner of folk-song. Cross checking and research has not proved easy. Many of the people who produce songs for small children have rearranged music and words, freely translated folk-songs from other countries, and worked independently on the same simple themes which would obviously prove attractive to children. Some songs and rhymes reveal their age, or newness, or place of origin by their subject matter, for example 'Wind the bobbin up' in most cases was contained only in the lists from Lancashire.

It was not the purpose of this book, however, to place and date the material but merely to produce a working collection of songs and rhymes to be of use whenever there are small children together. So many people say they have no musical ability that music has been indicated as simply as possible so that the songs can be sung. Most children and adults can use the dulcimer, chime bars or recorder found in the average home. Dulcimers may be made quite simply from mild steel strip by children, with a little adult help and strength. Once the tune has been learned, however, the human voice is the only instrument necessary, and the most unmusical of us transpose from key to key with neither trouble nor thought when singing.

I would like to thank all the teachers and nursery nurses who have helped make the collection, who have painstakingly copied out their own version of songs and rhymes for cross-reference purposes, or have allowed me to use their own original material. Thanks are also due to those authors, composers and publishers who have given permission for copyright material to be used. Every effort has been made to trace copyright but if any omissions have been made please let us know and we will gladly make acknowledgements in our next edition.

B. M.

Games to Play with a Baby

This little pig went to market,
This little pig stayed at home;
This little pig had roast beef,
This little pig had none.
This little pig cried, 'Wee–wee–wee,
I can't find my way home.'

Point to each toe in turn, starting with the big one,
and on the last line tickle underneath the baby's foot.

Slowly, slowly, very slowly
Creeps the garden snail.
Slowly, slowly, very slowly
Up the wooden rail.

Quickly, quickly, very quickly
Runs the little mouse.
Quickly, quickly, very quickly
Round about the house.

Use hands to mime the actions suggested by the words,
or play with the baby as a tickling game.

Round and round the garden
Run your index finger round the baby's palm.
Went the Teddy Bear,

One step,

Two steps,
'Jump' your finger up his arm.
Tickly under there.
Tickle him under his arm.

Round and round the haystack,
Went the little mouse,
One step,
Two steps,
In his little house.

Repeat the same actions for the second verse.

This is the father short and stout,
This is the mother with children all about.
This is the brother tall you see,
This is the sister with dolly on her knee.
This is the baby sure to grow,
And here is the family all in a row.

Point to each finger in turn, starting with the thumb.

Knock at the door,
Pretend to knock on the forehead.
Pull the bell,
Lightly pull a lock of hair.
Lift the latch,
Lightly pinch the nose.
And walk in.
Pretend to put your fingers on his mouth.

Use this as a feature play with a baby.

This little cow eats grass,
This little cow eats hay;
This little cow drinks water;
This little cow runs away;
This little cow does nothing
But just lies down all day.
We'll chase her,
We'll chase her,
We'll chase her away!

Point to each finger in turn, starting with the thumb.
Tickle the little finger and then up the baby's arm.

Pat-a-cake, pat-a-cake,
Baker's man,
Bake me a cake
As fast as you can.
Pat it and prick it
And mark it with B,
And put it in the oven
For Baby and me.

Use this for a hand-clapping game with a baby.
Use the traditional tune.

Ride a cock horse
To Banbury Cross,
To see a fine lady
Upon a white horse.
With rings on her fingers
And bells on her toes,
She shall have music
Wherever she goes.

Use this for a knee ride for a baby.
Use the traditional tune.

Trot, trot, trot,
Go and never stop.
Trudge along, my little pony,
Where 'tis rough and where 'tis stony.
Go and never stop,
Trot, trot, trot, trot, trot!

Use this for a knee ride for a baby, making the bounces fit in with the rhythm of the rhyme.

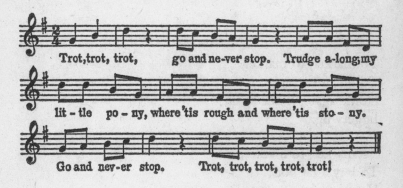

Two little eyes to look around,
Two little ears to hear each sound;
One little nose to smell what's sweet,
One little mouth that likes to eat.

Point to each feature as it is mentioned.

See-saw, Sacradown,
Which is the way
To London Town?
One foot up,
The other foot down,
That is the way
To London Town.

Use this for a knee ride for a baby.

To market, to market,
To buy a fat pig;
Home again, home again,
Jiggety jig.

To market, to market,
To buy a fat hog;
Home again, home again,
Joggety jog.

Say this while giving the baby a knee ride.

A farmer went trotting upon his grey mare,
Bumpety, bumpety, bump!
With his daughter behind him so rosy and fair,
Lumpety, lumpety, lump!

A magpie cried 'Caw,' and they all tumbled down,
Bumpety, bumpety, bump!
The mare broke her knees, and the farmer his crown,
Lumpety, lumpety, lump!

The mischievous magpie flew laughing away,
Bumpety, bumpety, bump!
And vowed he would serve them the same the next day,
Lumpety, lumpety, lump!

This rhyme may be used for knee rides or as a miming game.

Peek-a-boo, peek-a-boo,
Who's that hiding there?
Peek-a-boo, peek-a-boo,
Peter's behind the chair.

This may be played with a baby or by two older children playing together.

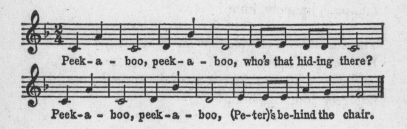

Peek-a - boo, peek-a - boo, who's that hid-ing there?

Peek-a - boo, peek-a - boo, (Pe-ter)'s be-hind the chair.

Shoe a little horse,
Shoe a little mare,
But let the little colt
Go bare, bare, bare.

Say this rhyme while patting a baby's feet.

Leg over leg
As the dog went to Dover,
When he came to a stile –
Jump, he went over.

*Cross your knees and sit the baby on one ankle, holding his hands.
Bounce him to the rhythm of the rhyme, and on 'Jump' give him a big
swing by uncrossing your knees.*

In the House

Here is a house built up high,
Stretch arms up, touching fingertips.
With two tall chimneys reaching the sky.
Stretch arms up separately.
Here are the windows,
Make square shape with hands.
Here is the door.
Knock.
If we peep inside, we'll see a mouse on
the floor.
Raise hands in fright.

Mix a pancake,
Stir a pancake,
Pop it in the pan.

Fry the pancake,
Toss the pancake,
Catch it if you can!

Mime the appropriate actions.

There's such a tiny little mouse,
Indicate how small he is with a thumb and forefinger.

Living safely in my house.
Place one forefinger into a clenched fist.

Out at night he'll softly creep,
Creep fingers slowly across the floor.

When everyone is fast asleep:
Rest head on folded hands.

But always in the light of day
Spread hands high and wide to represent sunrise.

He'll softly, softly creep away.
Creep fingers slowly back again to rest in the other hand.

Chop, chop, choppity-chop,
Cut off the bottom,
And cut off the top.
What there is left we will
Put in the pot;
Chop, chop, choppity-chop.

Children pretend to chop vegetables for soup.
Each child can suggest a vegetable that he knows.
Chopping movements are made with the side of
the hand in time to the words.

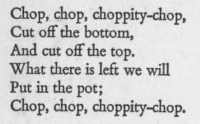

Here is a house,
Make an arch with fingertips.

With two little people.
Wriggle thumbs beneath the arch.

Quite close by is a church with a steeple.
Interlock fingers with tips of forefingers raised together.

They have a cat
Clench right hand, and raise thumb and little finger for ears.

With kittens four;
Hold up four fingers of the left hand.

See them scamper across the floor.
Run the fingers across the floor.

Slice, slice, the bread looks nice.
Spread, spread butter on the bread.
On the top put jam so sweet,
Now it's nice for us to eat.

Do the actions suggested by the words.

My little house won't stand up straight,
    Touch fingertips of both hands to make a roof,
    rocking from side to side.

My little house has lost its gate,
    Drop two little fingers.

My little house bends up and down,
    Rock hands violently from side to side.

My little house is the oldest one in town.
    Continue rocking hands.

Here comes the wind; it blows and blows
again.
    Blow through two thumbs.

Down falls my little house. Oh, what a
shame!
    Drop hands into lap.

This is my little house,
Indicate a roof by putting fingertips together.

This is the door.
Hold tips of index fingers together.

The windows are shining
Pretend to polish the windows.

And so is the floor.
Pretend to polish the floor.

Outside there is a chimney
Hold hands up high for the chimney.

As tall as can be,

With smoke that goes curling up.
Wave one hand slowly above head.

Come and see.

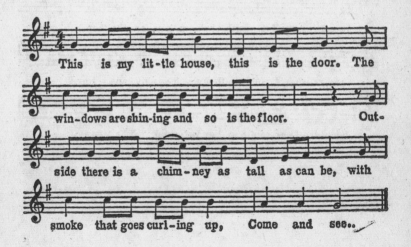

Five currant buns in a baker's shop,
Round and fat with sugar on the top.
Along came a boy with a penny one day,
Bought a currant bun and took it away.

Four currant buns, etc.

This may be played with fingers or by having five children represent the buns and another child the boy with the penny.

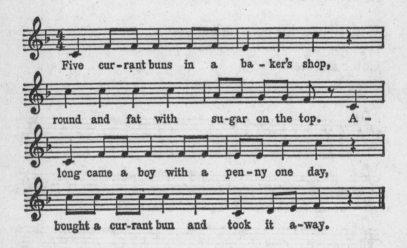

Five cur-rant buns in a ba-ker's shop,
round and fat with su-gar on the top. A-
long came a boy with a pen-ny one day,
bought a cur-rant bun and took it a-way.

I'm a little teapot, short and stout;
Children make themselves stout.

Here's my handle, here's my spout.
Put one hand on hip, hold out the other arm as a spout.

When I see the tea-cups, hear me shout,
Stand as above.

'Tip me up and pour me out.'
Tip slowly to the side of the outstretched arm.

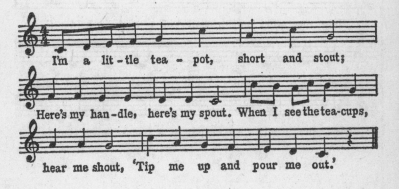

I'm a lit-tle tea-pot, short and stout; Here's my han-dle, here's my spout. When I see the tea-cups, hear me shout, 'Tip me up and pour me out.'

Help me wind my ball of wool,
Hold it gently, do not pull.
Wind the wool and wind the wool,
Around, around, around.

*Two children sit together, one pretending to
hold the wool, one pretending to wind.*

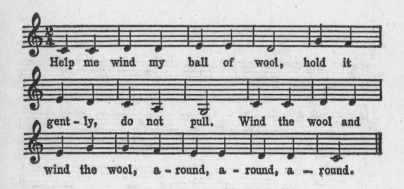

Build a house with five bricks,

One, two, three, four, five.
   Use clenched fists for bricks, putting one on top of the other five times.

Put a roof on top
   Raise both arms above head with fingers touching.

And a chimney too,
   Straighten arms.

Where the wind blows through . . .

WHOO WHOO.
   Blow hard (or whistle).

With my little broom I sweep, sweep, sweep;
On my little toes I creep, creep, creep.
With my little eyes I peep, peep, peep;
On my little bed I sleep, sleep, sleep.

Mime the actions suggested by the words.

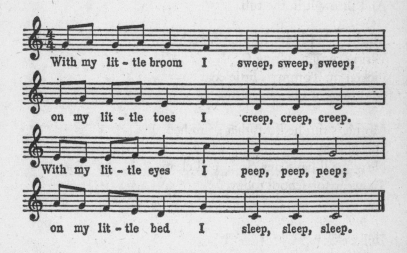

With my lit - tle broom I sweep, sweep, sweep;

on my lit - tle toes I creep, creep, creep.

With my lit - tle eyes I peep, peep, peep;

on my lit - tle bed I sleep, sleep, sleep.

Mother's washing, Mother's washing,
Rub, rub, rub.
Picked up Johnny's little shirt
And threw it in the tub.

Mother's washing, Mother's washing,
Scrub, scrub, scrub.
Picked up Mary's little frock
And threw it in the tub.

Mother's washing, Mother's washing,
Wring, wring, wring.
Picked up Tommy's little coat
And hung it on some string.

Mother's finished, Mother's finished,
Hip hooray!
Now we'll have our clothes all clean
To wear for school today.

Mime the actions suggested by the words.

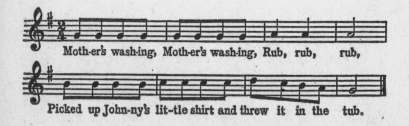

Moth-er's wash-ing, Moth-er's wash-ing, Rub, rub, rub,

Picked up John-ny's lit-tle shirt and threw it in the tub.

Up the tall white candle-stick
Make left arm into candle-stick.
Crept little Mousie Brown,
Two fingers of right hand run up candle-stick.
Right to the top but he couldn't get down.
Fingers stay at the top.
So he called to his Grandma,
Call through cupped hands.
'Grandma, Grandma,'

But Grandma was in town.

So he curled himself into a ball
Remake candle-stick, clench right fist.
— And rolled himself down.
Clench both fists and roll round each other moving downwards.

These are Grandmother's glasses,
This is Grandmother's hat;
Grandmother claps her hands like this,
And folds them in her lap.

These are Grandfather's glasses,
This is Grandfather's hat;
This is the way he folds his arms,
And has a little nap.

Make appropriate actions to fit the words, joining forefinger and thumb to make the spectacles. Use a deeper voice for the second verse.

Here are the lady's knives and forks,
Interlace fingers, palms upwards.

Here is the lady's table;
Turn hands over with fingers still interlaced.

Here is the lady's looking glass,
Raise two forefingers to a point.

And here is the baby's cradle.
*Raise two little fingers to a point to make the
other end of the cradle, and rock hands.*

I have a little cuckoo clock,

It sits all day and says 'Tick-tock';
Use one arm as a pendulum.

It has a little roof like this,
Make a roof over head using arms.

And underneath a birdie sits.

And when the clock strikes 'One',
Nod head once from under roof.

The bird comes out and says 'Cuckoo'.

*Subsequent verses: The clock strikes 'One, two' 'One, two, three' . . .
The head is nodded the appropriate number of times.*

This is the way we wash our clothes,
Rub-a-dub-dub, rub-a-dub-dub.
Watch them getting clean and white,
Rub-a-dub-dub, rub-a-dub-dub!

This is the way we mangle them,
Rumble-de-dee, rumble-de-dee.
Round and round the handle goes,
Rumble-de-dee, rumble-de-dee!

This is the way we hang them out,
Flippity-flap, flippity-flap.
See them blowing in the wind,
Flippity-flap, flippity-flap!

This is the way we iron them,
Smooth as smooth can be!
Soon our wash day will be done,
Then we'll have our tea.

Mime the actions suggested by the words.
Use the tune 'Here we go round the mulberry bush'.

Mummy has scissors, snip, snip, snip;
Mummy has cotton, stitch, stitch, stitch.
Mummy has buttons, one, two, three;
She's making a dress,
Just for me!

Mime the actions suggested by the words.

What does the clock in the hall say?
Tick, tock, tick, tock.
What does the clock in the room say?
Tick, tick, tick, tick, tick, tick, tick, tick.
What do little watches all say?
Tick-a, tick-a, tick-a, tick-a, tick-a, tick-a, tick.

Place the hands together and use them to indicate the pendulum of the clocks.

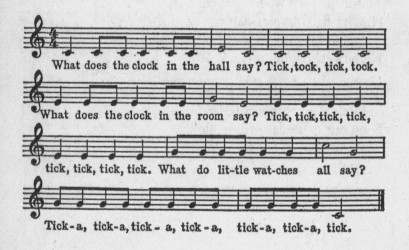

What does the clock in the hall say? Tick, tock, tick, tock.

What does the clock in the room say? Tick, tick, tick, tick,

tick, tick, tick, tick. What do lit-tle wat-ches all say?

Tick-a, tick-a, tick-a, tick-a, tick-a, tick-a, tick.

In the Garden

Oh, what shall we do in our garden this fine day?
Oh, what shall we do in our garden this fine day?
We'll dig and dig and dig well,
With our spades this way.
Oh, we'll dig and we'll dig in our garden this fine day.

*Mime the actions suggested by the words. Other activities may be suggested
by the children.*
Tune: 'The Bluebells of Scotland'.

A tiny, tiny worm
Wriggled along the ground
It wriggled along like this
Without a sound.

It came to a tiny hole,
A tiny hole in the ground,
It wriggled right inside,
Without a sound.

Wriggle right index finger along the floor.
Make the hole with left thumb and index finger.

To and fro, to and fro,
Sweeping with my broom I go.
All the fallen leaves I sweep,
In a big and tidy heap.

Mime the actions suggested by the words.

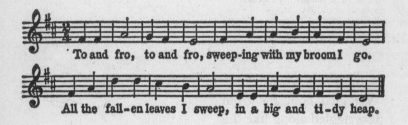

To and fro, to and fro, sweep-ing with my broom I go.
All the fall-en leaves I sweep, in a big and ti-dy heap.

What do you suppose?

A bee sat on my nose.
Land the tips of finger and thumb, touching, on the bridge of the nose.
Then what do you think?

He gave me a wink
Wink one eye.
And said, 'I beg your pardon,

I thought you were the garden.'
Make flying-away movements with hand.

Here is the beehive.
Where are the bees?
Hiding where nobody sees.

Watch them come creeping
Out of their hive;
One and two and three, four, five.

1st verse: Make a beehive with two hands, fingers interlocked.
2nd verse: 'Creep' the fingers of one hand out of the other,
then make them fly about.

Flowers grow like this,
   Cup hands.
Trees grow like this;
   Spread arms.
I grow
   Jump up and stretch.
Just like that!

Five little peas in a pea-pod pressed,
   Clench fingers on one hand.
One grew, two grew and so did all the rest.
   Raise fingers slowly.
They grew and grew and did not stop,
   Stretch fingers wide.
Until one day the pod went POP.
   Clap loudly on POP.

How does a caterpillar go?
Dear me, does anybody know?
How does a caterpillar go?
On a cabbage leaf the whole day long.

How does a little froggie go? etc.
By a lily pond the whole day long.

How does a fluffy duckling go? etc.
A-searching worms the whole day long.

Mime suitable actions for each animal.

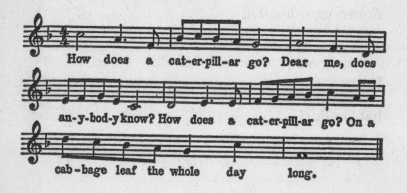

How does a cat-er-pill-ar go? Dear me, does an-y-bod-y know? How does a cat-er-pill-ar go? On a cab-bage leaf the whole day long.

Old Tom Tomato, like a red ball,

Basked in the sunshine by the garden wall.
    Make fist into a ball.

Along came — with his mouth open wide

And old Tom Tomato popped inside.
    Open mouth and put fingers in.

Down, down, down, down the red lane —
    Stroke throat.

We won't see old Tom Tomato again.

But — chuckled and said 'Ha ha!

I like red tomatoes, please give me some
    more.'
        Hold out hand.

Here we go round the mulberry bush,
The mulberry bush, the mulberry bush,
Here we go round the mulberry bush,
On a cold and frosty morning.

This is the way we sweep the floor, etc.

This is the way we scrub the clothes, etc.

During the first verse the children skip round in a ring.
They will suggest more actions for themselves.
Use the traditional tune.

I had a little cherry stone

And put it in the ground,
Pretend to put cherry in left hand using right thumb and forefinger.

And when next year I went to look,

A tiny shoot I found.
Right forefinger 'grows' up from clenched left fist.

The shoot grew upwards day by day,
Both hands rise upwards.

And soon became a tree.

I picked the rosy cherries then,
Right hand stays up as tree, and left hand picks cherries.

And ate them for my tea.

Here is a tree with its leaves so green,
Stretch arms out.

Here are the apples that hang between,
Clench fists.

When the wind blows the apples will fall.
Drop arms.

Here is a basket to gather them all.
Interlock fingers.

Ring a ring o' roses,
A pocket full of posies,
A-tishoo, a-tishoo,
We all fall down.

The king has sent his daughter
To fetch a pail of water,
A-tishoo, a-tishoo,
We all fall down.

The robin on the steeple
Is singing to the people,
A-tishoo, a-tishoo,
We all fall down.

All the children skip round in a ring and sit down quickly on 'A-tishoo'.
Use the traditional tune.

We are going to plant a bean,
Plant a bean, plant a bean;
We are going to plant a bean,
In our little garden green.

First we plant it with our finger, etc.

Then the little bean will grow, etc.

Then the summer sun will shine, etc.

Then the winter winds will blow, etc.

Then the little bean will die, etc.

Mime the actions suggested by the words.
Use the tune: 'Here we go round the mulberry bush'.

Six little snails
> *Use fingers to indicate the number of snails.*

Lived in a tree.
> *Raise arms for branches.*

Johnny threw a stone
> *Indicate how large the stone was.*

And down came three.
> *Use fingers to show how many fell.*

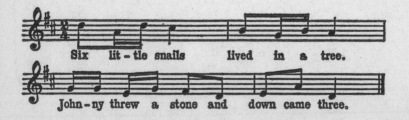

Rhymes and Songs about Toys

Here's a ball for baby,
Make a ball with cupped hands.
Big and soft and round.

Here is baby's hammer,
Hammer with one fist.
See how he can pound.

Here is baby's music,
Clap hands.
Clapping, clapping, so.

Here are baby's soldiers,
Hold fingers up straight.
Standing in a row.

Here is her umbrella,
Hold hands above head.
To keep our baby dry.

Here is baby's cradle,
Fold arms together and rock them.
To rock-a-baby-bye.

Here is a box;
> *Make a box with one fist lightly clenched.*

Put on the lid.
> *Use the other hand for a lid.*

I wonder whatever inside is hid?
> *Peep under the lid.*

Why, it's a — without any doubt.
> *Poke one finger through the clenched fist.*

Open the box and let it come out!
> *Open the fist. Make the appropriate noise for*
> *whatever object was named.*

Suggestions for what is inside the box can include anything
which makes a distinctive noise.

What have I got in my toy shop today,
Toy shop today, toy shop today;
What have I got in my toy shop today?
You tell me.

The adult sings the verse and points to one child who must suggest a toy.
The children all mime the action of the toy.
Use the tune for 'Here we go round the mulberry bush'.

Miss Polly had a dolly
Fold arms together and pretend to rock the dolly.
Who was sick, sick, sick.

So she phoned for the doctor
Put one hand to an ear and one to the mouth.
To be quick, quick, quick.

The doctor came
Swing one arm like a doctor carrying a bag.
With his bag and his hat,

And he rapped at the door
Knock on the floor.
With a rat-tat-tat.

He looked at the dolly

And he shook his head.
Shake head gravely.
Then he said, 'Miss Polly,

Put her straight to bed.'

He wrote on a paper
Write on the palm of one hand with forefinger.
For a pill, pill, pill;

'I'll be back in the morning
Wave good-bye.
With my bill, bill, bill.'

I'm a fairy doll on the Christmas tree;
Boys and girls come and look at me.
Look at me, see what I can do;
Then all of you can do it too.

Each child has a turn at choosing which toy to be and miming an action which the other children imitate. Hum or 'la-la' to the verse music while all the children imitate the action.

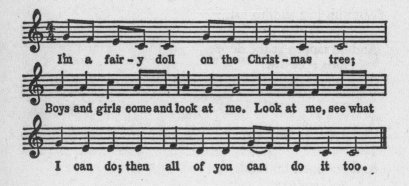

I'm a fair-y doll   on the Christ-mas   tree;

Boys and girls come and look at   me. Look at   me, see what

I   can do; then   all   of you can   do   it too.

See each India rubber ball,
Bouncing is not hard at all;
Bouncing, bouncing, bouncing, bouncing,
Is not hard at all.

Use this as a jumping or skipping rhyme.

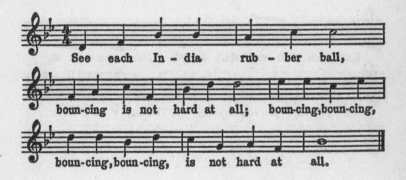

Have you seen my dolly?
Have you seen my dolly?
Have you seen my dolly?
The dolly in the box?

Adult pretends to take a dolly from the box and describes it (e.g. black crinkly hair, striped trousers). The children guess what it is and mime the action they think it would make.

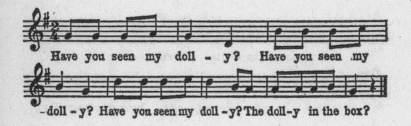

Have you seen my doll - y? Have you seen my
-doll - y? Have you seen my doll - y? The doll-y in the box?

This is how the snowflakes play about,
Up in cloudland they dance in and out.

This is how they whirl down the street,
Powdering everybody they meet.

This is how they come fluttering down,
Whitening the roads, the fields and the town.

This is how the snowflakes cover the trees,
Each branch and twig bends in the breeze.

This is how they cover the ground,
Cover it thickly, with never a sound.

This is how snowflakes blow in a heap,
Looking just like fleecy sheep.

This is how people shiver and shake
On a snowy morning when they first awake.

This is how snowflakes melt away
When the sun sends out his beams to play.

Use fingers, arms and body to mime the actions suggested by the words.

I hear thunder, I hear thunder;
Drum the feet on the floor.
Hark, don't you, hark, don't you?
Pretend to listen.
Pitter-patter raindrops,
Indicate rain with fingers.
Pitter-patter raindrops,

I'm wet through –
Shake the whole body vigorously.
SO ARE YOU!
Point to a neighbour.

To the tune of 'Frère Jacques'.

Softly, softly falling so,
This is how the snowflakes go.
Pitter-patter, pitter-patter,
Pit pit pat,
Down go the raindrops
On my hat.

Use hands to mime the actions suggested by the words.

The autumn leaves have fallen down,
Fallen down, fallen down;
The wind he came and blew them round,
And blew them around.

Let's find a brush and start to sweep,
Start to sweep, start to sweep,
And make them into a great big heap,
Into a great big heap.

Then light the bonfire and burn them away,
Burn them away, burn them away;
And now it's tidy we'll dance and play,
We'll dance and play.

Do the actions suggested by the words.

The au - tumn leaves have fall - en down, fall - en down, fall - en down; The wind he came and blew them round, and blew___ them a - round.

Pray open your umbrella,
Pray open your umbrella,
Pray open your umbrella,
And shield me from the rain.

The shower is nearly over,
The shower is nearly over,
The shower is nearly over,
So shut it up again.

Small movements may be made with the hands,
or the arms may be used for large actions.

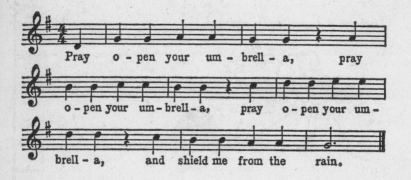

Pray o - pen your um - brell - a, pray
o - pen your um - brell - a, pray o - pen your um -
brell - a, and shield me from the rain.

Things We See in the Town

Here is the church,
Interlace fingers with knuckles showing upwards.
Here is the steeple,
Point index fingers up together to make a steeple.
Open the doors
Turn hands over with fingers still interlaced.
And here are the people.
Wriggle fingertips.
Here's the parson going upstairs,
Make a ladder with the left hand and walk right thumb and index finger up.
And here he is a-saying his prayers.
Put hands together as for prayer.

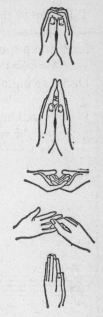

Here is a steamroller, rolling and rolling,
Ever so slowly, because of its load.
Then it rolls up to the top of the hill,
Puffing and panting it has to stand still.
Then it rolls . . . all the way down!

*Roll fists round each other, slowly moving upwards,
then down again very fast on the last line.*

Tall shop in the town,
>*Use arms to make a 'roof' over the head.*

Lifts moving up and down.
>*Move clenched fists up and down in opposite directions.*

Doors swinging round about,
>*Move fists round each other.*

People walking in and out.
>*Move fists forwards and backwards
>crossing each other.*

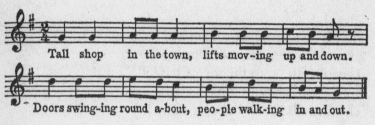

Tall shop in the town, lifts mov-ing up and down.

Doors swing-ing round a-bout, peo-ple walk-ing in and out.

Down by the station, early in the morning,
See the little puffer trains all in a row.
See the engine driver pull the little handle.
Choo, choo, choo, and off we go.

Down at the farmyard early in the morning,
See the little tractor standing in the barn.
Do you see the farmer pull the little handle?
Chug, chug, chug, and off we go.

More verses can be added as children suggest different vehicles.
For each verse mime the action suggested by each vehicle.

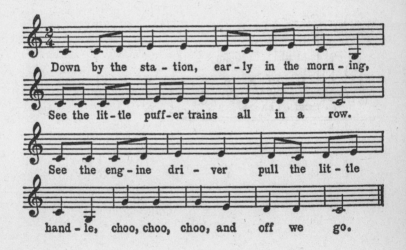

Down by the sta - tion, ear - ly in the morn - ing,
See the lit - tle puff - er trains all in a row.
See the eng - ine dri - ver pull the lit - tle
hand - le, choo, choo, choo, and off we go.

Piggy on the railway,
Picking up stones;
Along came an engine
And broke poor Piggy's bones.

'Oh!' said Piggy,
'That's not fair.'
'Oh!' said the engine driver,
'I don't care!'

1st verse: One fist represents Piggy and the other the engine.
2nd verse: Shake one finger admonishingly, then give a big shrug.

The train is carrying coal.
It has ten trucks you'll find;
At every station the train will stop
And leave (two) trucks behind.

The children make a long train and 'shunt' round the room. At the end of each verse the previously agreed number of 'trucks' are left behind, and the train goes on again until only one child is left.

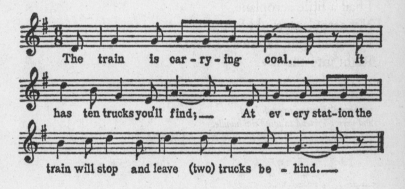

One red engine puffing down the track,
One red engine puffing, puffing back.
Two red engines puffing down the track,
Etc.

This may be played with fingers or by children making a train and one child joining in at each verse.

I had a little engine,
But it wouldn't go;
I had to push and push and push,
But still it wouldn't go.

I had a little motor-car,
But it wouldn't go;
I had to wind and wind and wind,
But still it wouldn't go.

I had a little aeroplane,
My aeroplane could fly;
I jumped right in, away I flew,
Right into the sky.

1st verse: Pretend to push hard.
2nd verse: Pretend to wind the handle.
3rd verse: Run round the room with arms outstretched.

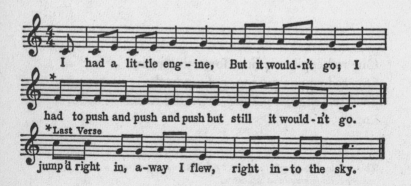

Here comes a policeman riding on a bicycle,
Ting, ling, ling, keep the roadway clear.
When I am older I shall ride a bicycle,
Ting, ling, ling, keep the roadway clear.

Here comes a policeman, driving in a motor-car,
Peep, peep, peep, keep the roadway clear.
When I am older I shall drive a motor-car,
Peep, peep, peep, keep the roadway clear.

*Children move round the room raising feet high to represent the pedalling,
hands held as if on handlebars.
For the second verse they move round quickly holding hands and arms as if steering.*

Aeroplanes, aeroplanes all in a row;
Aeroplanes, aeroplanes ready to go.
Hark, they're beginning to buzz and to hum,
Bzzzzz;
Engines all working so come along, come.
Now we are flying up into the sky,
Faster and faster, oh, ever so high.

Children lie face down on the floor making a buzzing noise, then stand up and pretend to fly round the room.

The wheels on the bus go round and round,
Round and round, round and round.
The wheels on the bus go round and round,
All day long.

The horn on the bus goes peep, peep, peep, etc.

The windscreen wiper on the bus goes swish, swish, swish, etc.

The people on the bus bounce up and down, etc.

Mime the actions suggested by the words. Other situations may be suggested by the children.

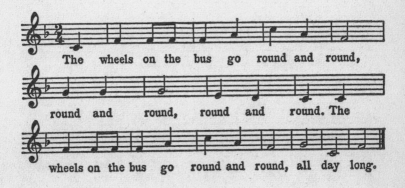

The wheels on the bus go round and round, round and round, round and round. The wheels on the bus go round and round, all day long.

Here comes a big red bus,
A big red bus, a big red bus;
Here comes a big red bus,
To take us to the shops.

Here comes a mini bus, etc.
To take us all to school.

Here comes a motor-car, etc.
To take us to the sea.

1st verse: Move ponderously about the room.
2nd verse: Move fairly fast about the room.
3rd verse: Run very fast round the room.
May be sung to the tune of 'Jack and Jill'.

I went to visit a farm one day;
I saw a (cow) across the way,
And what d'you think I heard it say?
MOO, MOO, MOO.

Repeat using different animals.

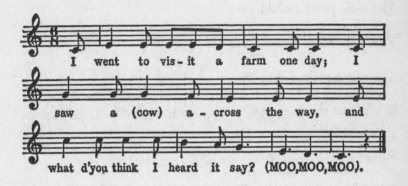

One man went to mow,
Went to mow a meadow;
One man and his dog, Bow-wow,
Went to mow a meadow.

Two men went to mow, etc.

Three men, etc.

Four men, etc.

*This may be played as a finger counting game, or with children acting as the men.
Use the traditional tune.*

The farmer's in his dell,
The farmer's in his dell,
E...I...E...I
The farmer's in his dell.

The farmer picks a wife, etc.

The wife picks a child, etc.

The child picks a nurse, etc.

The nurse picks a dog, etc.

We all pat the dog, etc.

One child is chosen to be the farmer and stands in a ring formed by the other children. During the first verse the ring moves slowly round the 'farmer' as they sing. During the second verse the 'farmer' chooses a girl to stand with him as a 'wife'. During the third verse the wife chooses someone to be a 'child'. This is repeated with each character until in the last verse all the children pat the 'dog'. Use the traditional tune.

Little piggy-wig on the farm close by,
All by himself ran away from the sty.
The dog said 'Woof',
The cow said 'Moo',
The sheep said 'Baa',
The dove said 'Coo',
Little piggy-wig began to cry,
And as fast as he could he ran back to the sty.

Mime the actions suggested by the words.

Old McDonald had a farm,
E...I...E...I...O
And on that farm he had some cows,
E...I...E...I...O
With a moo-moo here,
And a moo-moo there,
Here a moo,
There a moo,
Everywhere a moo-moo,
Old McDonald had a farm,
E...I...E...I...O

Each time the verse is sung a different animal is named
and the new sound is incorporated into the chorus as follows:

With a quack-quack here,
And a quack-quack there,
Here a quack,
There a quack,
Everywhere a quack-quack;
With a moo-moo here,
And a moo-moo there,
Here a moo,
There a moo,
Everywhere a moo-moo,
Old McDonald had a farm,
E...I...E...I...O

Very small children may not be able to manage too long a chorus,
in which case only the animal mentioned in the verse is included.
Use the traditional tune.

Three little pigs and a little pig more
Knocked on the farmer's bright green door:
'Be quick, Mr Farmer, we want our lunch,
Hunch, hunch, hunch!'

Three little calves and a little calf more
Knocked on the farmer's bright green door:
'Be quick, Mr Farmer, we want our lunch too,
Moo, moo, moo!'

The farmer came out with a furious roar:
'Who's that a-hammering at my door?
Not a bit, not a scrap will you get from me.'
Thus said he.

Those poor little animals knocked once more,
Quietly, quietly on the door,
And said most politely on their knees,
'If you please!'

Hold up the right number of fingers to represent the animals
and knock loudly on the floor as indicated by the words.

Have you seen the little ducks
Swimming in the water?
Mother, father, baby ducks,
Grand-mamma and daughter.

Have you seen them dip their bills,
Swimming in the water?, etc.

Have you seen them flap their wings,
Swimming in the water?, etc.

Do the actions suggested by the words.

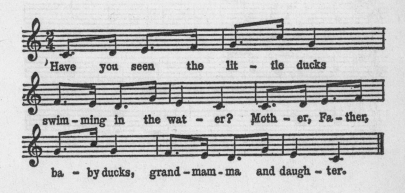

(One) little cockerel bright and gay
Stood on a gate at break of day.
'Ho, little cockerel, how do you do?'
'Quite well, thank you. Cock-a-doodle-doo.'

*Repeat with two cockerels, etc. The children acting as cockerels stand on one foot
with hands on hips to represent wings and sing the last line alone.*

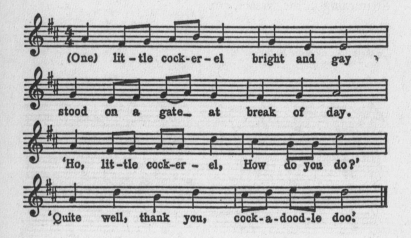

Oats and beans and barley grow,
Oats and beans and barley grow,
But not you nor I nor anyone know
How oats and beans and barley grow.

First the farmer sows his seed,
Then he stands and takes his ease,
Stamps his feet and claps his hands
And turns him round to view the land.

*During the first verse the children skip round in a ring. During the second verse
they do the appropriate actions. (There are more verses to this but they are not so
attractive to small children as the first two.)*

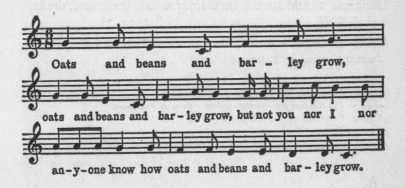

If I could have a windmill, a windmill, a windmill,
If I could have a windmill, I know what I would do.

I'd have it pump some water, some water, some water,
I'd have it pump some water all up from the river below.

And then I'd have a duckpond, a duckpond, a duckpond,
And then I'd have a duckpond, for ducks and geese to swim.

The ducks would make their wings flap, their wings flap,
   their wings flap,
The ducks would make their wings flap, and then they
   would say 'Quack, quack.'

The geese would stretch their long necks, their long necks,
   their long necks,
The geese would stretch their long necks, and then they
   would answer 's-s-s-s !'

1st verse: Stretch out both arms and swing them round.
2nd verse: Put clenched fists together and raise them up and down.
3rd verse: Pretend to scoop a hole in the ground.
4th verse: Put hands on hips and waggle elbows.
5th verse: Lower and raise heads stretching necks as far as possible.

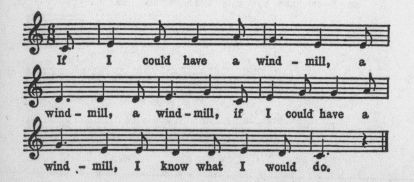

If I could have a wind - mill, a
wind - mill, a wind - mill, if I could have a
wind - mill, I know what I would do.

Do you plant your cabbages
In the right way, in the right way?
Do you plant your cabbages
In the right way if you please?

You can plant them with your hand
With your hand, with your hand;
You can plant them with your hand
In the right way if you please.

You can plant them with your fork,
                              spade,
                              foot,
                              knee,
                              elbow,
                              head,
                              nose, etc.

During the first verse the children skip round in a ring. During the following verses they do the actions suggested by the words. All kinds of suggestions will be made by the children.

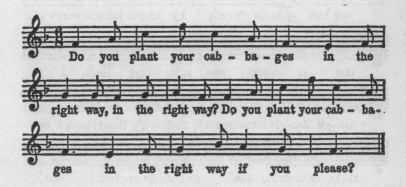

Do you plant your cab-ba-ges in the right way, in the right way? Do you plant your cab-ba-ges in the right way if you please?

When all the cows were sleeping,
And the sun had gone to bed,
Up jumped the scarecrow,
And this is what he said:

'I'm a dingle dangle scarecrow
With a flippy floppy hat.
I can shake my hands like this,
And shake my feet like that.'

When all the hens were roosting,
And the moon behind a cloud,
Up jumped the scarecrow
And shouted very loud:

'I'm a dingle dangle scarecrow,' etc.

Children mime the actions suggested by the words.

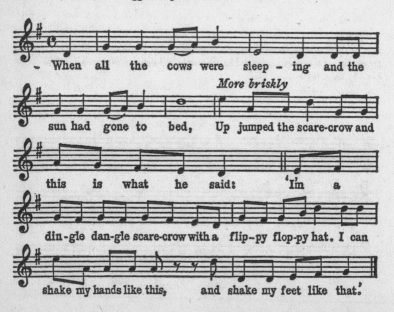

Five little leaves so bright and gay
Were dancing about on a tree one day.
The wind came blowing through the town
oooooo...oooooo...
One little leaf came tumbling down.

Four little leaves so bright and gay, etc.

Use fingers to represent leaves, and blow hard to make the noise of the wind.

Put your finger in Foxy's hole.
Foxy's not at home.
Foxy's out at the back door
A-picking at a bone.

Clench hand, put finger through.

Whisky Frisky,
Hipperty hop,
Up he goes
To the tree top.

Whirly, twirly,
Round and round,
Down he scampers
To the ground.

Furly curly,
What a tail;
Tall as a feather,
Broad as a sail.

Where's his supper?
In the shell,
Snappy, cracky,
Out it fell.

Use hands and arms to suggest the squirrel's movements.

Ten little squirrels sat on a tree.
Show ten fingers.
The first two said, 'Why, what do we see?'
Hold up thumbs.
The next two said, 'A man with a gun.'
Hold up forefingers.
The next two said, 'Let's run, let's run.'
Hold up middle fingers.
The next two said, 'Let's hide in the shade,'
Hold up ring fingers.
The next two said, 'Why, we're not afraid,'
Hold up the little fingers.
But BANG went the gun, and away they all ran.
Clap loudly and hide all fingers.

This little rabbit said, 'Let's play.'
This little rabbit said, 'In the hay.'
This little rabbit said, 'I see a man with a gun.'
This little rabbit said, 'That isn't fun.'
This little rabbit said, 'I'm off for a run.'
BANG went the gun,
And they all ran away,
And they never came back for a year and a day.

Point to all fingers and thumb in turn. Clap hands at BANG,
and hide fingers behind back.

We are woodmen sawing trees,
Sawing, sawing, sawing trees.
We don't stop for wind or weather,
We keep sawing all together;
We are woodmen sawing trees,
Sawing, sawing, sawing trees.

The tree falls down with a great big crash.
Now we all will take an axe,
And chop and chop with all our might,
To get some wood for the fire to light;
We are woodmen sawing trees,
Sawing, sawing, sawing trees.

Now we carry logs along,
Singing gaily this merry song;
Tra la la la la la la, etc.

Mime the actions suggested by the words.

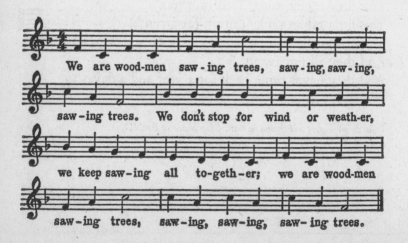

We are wood-men saw-ing trees, saw-ing, saw-ing,
saw-ing trees. We don't stop for wind or weath-er,
we keep saw-ing all to-geth-er; we are wood-men
saw-ing trees, saw-ing, saw-ing, saw-ing trees.

Here's a tree with trunk so brown.
Here I stand and chop it down.
Swing the chopper to and fro,
To and fro, to and fro;
Swing the chopper to and fro,
And chop the big tree down.

One child pretends to be the tree and his partner the woodman.

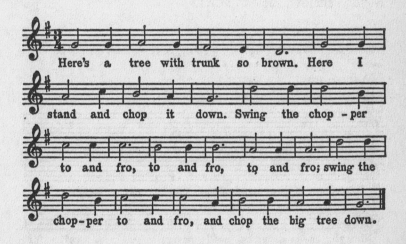

Here's a tree with trunk so brown. Here I stand and chop it down. Swing the chop-per to and fro, to and fro, to and fro; swing the chop-per to and fro, and chop the big tree down.

I know a little pussy,
Her coat is silver grey;
She lives down in the meadow,
Not very far away.
Although she is a pussy,
She'll never be a cat,
For she's a pussy willow –
Now what do you think of that?
Meiow, meiow, meiow, meiow,
Meiow, meiow, meiow, SCAT!

Children start from a crouch position, rise slowly, then come down again on the 'meiows', and jump up again on SCAT.

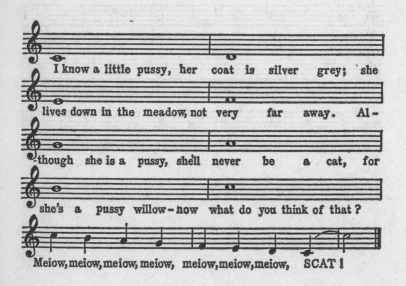

Down in the grass, curled up in a heap,
Lies a big snake, fast asleep.
When he hears the grasses blow,
He moves his body to and fro.
Up and down and in and out,
See him slowly move about!
Now his jaws are open, so –
Snap! He's caught my finger! Oh!

Use one arm resting on a table to represent the snake. Make his head by touching the thumb to the fingertip.

Down in the grass, curled up in a heap,
lies a big snake, fast a-sleep. When he hears the
grass-es blow, he moves his bo-dy to and fro.
Up and down and in and out,— See him slow-ly
move a-bout.— Now his jaws are o-pen so,
Snap! He's caught my fin-ger! Oh!

If you were a beech tree,
What would you do?
I'd grow and grow and grow so high,
Until I almost reached the sky,
I reached the sky!

Repeat naming different trees.
Indicate the shapes of the trees, for example hands above heads for beech trees,
arms held wide for pine trees, arms drooping for willow trees.

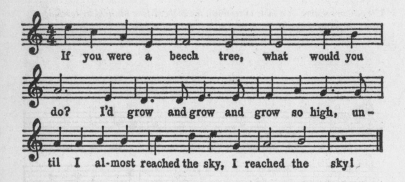

If you were a beech tree, what would you
do? I'd grow and grow and grow so high, until I al-most reached the sky, I reached the sky!

Four scarlet berries
Left upon the tree.
'Thanks,' said the blackbird,
'These will do for me.'
He ate numbers one and two,
Then ate number three;
When he'd eaten number four,
There was none to see!

Use four fingers on right hand for berries and left hand for blackbird.

The Zoo

Five little monkeys walked along the shore;
One went a-sailing,
Then there were four.
Four little monkeys climbed up a tree;
One of them tumbled down,
Then there were three.
Three little monkeys found a pot of glue;
One got stuck in it,
Then there were two.
Two little monkeys found a currant bun;
One ran away with it,
Then there was one.
One little monkey cried all afternoon,
So they put him in an aeroplane
And sent him to the moon.

Use fingers to indicate the number of monkeys.

Walking through the jungle,
What did I see?
A big lion roaring
At me, me, me!

Walking through the jungle,
What did I see?
A baby monkey laughing
At me, me, me!

Walking through the jungle,
What did I see?
A slippery snake hissing
At me, me, me!

*More animals may be added. Pretend to walk very carefully through the jungle,
and mime the actions to suggest each animal.*

Isn't it funny that a bear likes honey?
Buzz, buzz, buzz, I wonder why he does!
Go to sleep, Mr Bear.

Wake up, Mr Bear.

*Children sit in a circle with the child who is the bear in the centre with a small pot
beside him. During the first three lines the bear pretends to eat the honey, then goes
to sleep. A second child tries to pick up the pot but as soon as he touches it the
children shout 'wake up, Mr Bear', and the 'bear' chases this thief, who must try
to get round the circle and back to his place before the bear touches him.*

Here is the ostrich straight and tall,
Raise arm, fingers drooping.
Nodding his head above us all.

Here is the long snake on the ground,
Wriggle hand and arm.
Wriggling upon the stones he found.

Here are the birds that fly so high,
Flap arms.
Spreading their wings across the sky.

Here is the hedgehog, prickly, small,
Clench hand.
Rolling himself into a ball.

Here is the spider scuttling around,
Walk fingers like a spider.
Treading so lightly on the ground.

Here are the children fast asleep,
Pillow head on hands.
And here at night the owls do peep.
Make spectacles of thumbs and forefingers.

I saw a slippery, slithery snake
Slide through the grasses, making them shake.
Right index finger weaves through fingers of left hand.
He looked at me with his beady eye.
Right index finger and thumb make ring round eye.
'Go away from my pretty green garden,' said I.
Make shooing movements with left hand.
'ssssss,' said the slippery, slithery snake,
As he slid through the grasses making them shake.
Repeat first movement.

Let's see the monkeys climbing up a tree,
One, two, three, one, two, three.
Look, they're coming down again,
Isn't it fun?
Three, two, one, three, two, one.
Now we see the brown bears walk along the floor,
Two, three, four, two, three four.
Look out I see a tiger,
He might catch you!
Four, three, two, four, three, two.

Move hands up and down for the monkeys and straight along for the bears.
Both hands are held up for the tiger, and after being pointed on the word 'you'
are quickly hidden behind the back.

An elephant goes like this and that.
  Pat knees.

He's terrible big,
  Hands up high.

And he's terrible fat.
  Hands out wide.

He has no fingers,
  Wriggle fingers.

And he has no toes,
  Touch toes.

But goodness gracious, what a nose!
  Make curling movement away from nose.

The elephant is big and strong;
His ears are large, his trunk is long.
He walks around with heavy tread,
His keeper walking at his head.

Walk round very slowly, swinging from side to side; head bent down and one arm hanging down as the trunk.

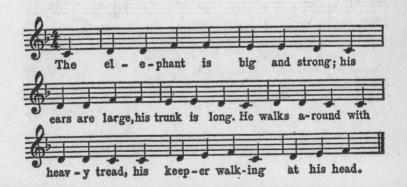

Look at the terrible crocodile,
I-oh, I-oh, I-oh.
He's swimming down the River Nile,
I-oh, I-oh, I-oh.

See his jaws are open wide,
I-oh, I-oh, I-oh.
A dear little fish is swimming inside . . .
Oh, no he isn't – (*This line is said softly*)
He's going the other way!

*Put palms flat together and weave them about for the crocodile. Keep the hands
touching at the wrist while finger tips flap apart in time to the refrain of 'I–oh'.
Use a wriggling finger for the little fish.*

Jump-jump! Kangaroo Brown,
Jump-jump! Off to town;
Jump-jump! Up hill and down,
Jump-jump! Kangaroo Brown.

Children make long slow jumps to the rhythm of the words.

Things We See Near Water

Puffer train, Puffer train,
Noisy little Puffer train.
If you're going to the sea,
Puffer train, Oh please take me.
Ff–Ff–Ff, Sh–Sh–Sh
Ch–Ch–Ch–Ch–Ch, Ch–Ch–Ch,
Noisy little Puffer train.

All the children make a long train and shunt round the floor.

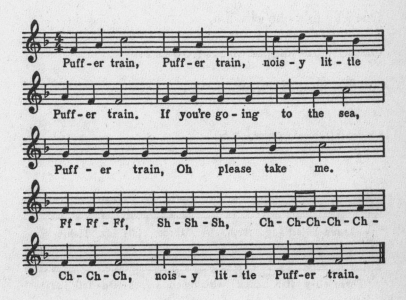

Puff-er train, Puff-er train, nois-y lit-tle

Puff-er train. If you're go-ing to the sea,

Puff - er train, Oh please take me.

Ff - Ff - Ff, Sh - Sh - Sh, Ch - Ch-Ch-Ch - Ch -

Ch - Ch - Ch, nois-y lit-tle Puff-er train.

Three jelly fish, three jelly fish,
Three jelly fish – sitting on a rock.
One fell off!... oooooo oooooo.

Two jelly fish, etc.

One jelly fish, etc.

No jelly fish, etc.

One jelly fish, one jelly fish,

One jelly fish jumped on ... HOORAY!

Another jumped on, etc.

Use fingers to show how many jelly fish.

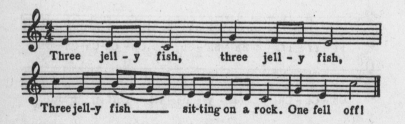

Three   jell - y   fish,   three   jell - y   fish,

Three jell-y fish_____   sit-ting on a rock. One fell   off!

I love to row in my big blue boat,
My big blue boat, my big blue boat;
I love to row in my big blue boat,
Out on the deep blue sea.

My big blue boat has two red sails,
Two red sails, two red sails;
My big blue boat has two red sails,
Two red sails.

So come for a row in my big blue boat,
My big blue boat, my big blue boat;
So come for a row in my big blue boat,
Out on the deep blue sea.

1st and 3rd verses: Pretend to row sitting on the floor. (Two children can sit facing each other holding hands and pulling backwards and forwards.)
2nd verse: Raise arms above the head and wave them gently like sails.

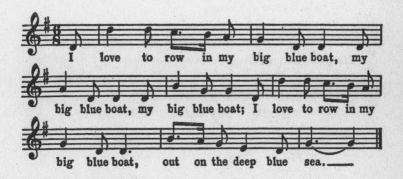

One, two, three, four, five
Count on fingers
Once I caught a fish alive
Wriggle hand like a fish
Six, seven, eight, nine, ten
Count fingers
Then I let him go again.
Pretend to throw fish back
Why did you let him go?
Because he bit my finger so.
Shake hand violently
Which finger did he bite?
This little finger on the right.
Hold up little finger on right hand.

Use the traditional tune.

Here is the sea, the wavy sea,
Indicate small waves with hands.
Here is the boat and here is me.
Lightly clench one fist for the boat, and pop one finger through for 'me'.
All the little fishes down below
Put hands down low.
Wriggle their tails, and away they all go.
Wriggle fingers then put them behind you.

The big ship sails through the Alley, Alley O,
Alley, Alley O, Alley, Alley O;
The big ship sails through the Alley, Alley O
On the last day of September.

The Captain said, 'It will never, never do,
Never, never do, never, never do,' etc.

The big ship sank to the bottom of the sea,
The bottom of the sea, the bottom of the sea, etc.

We all dip our heads in the deep blue sea,
The deep blue sea, the deep blue sea, etc.

All the children hold hands in a long line. One of the end children puts his arm up against a wall to make an arch. The child at the other end of the line goes under the arch followed by the others. As the last one goes through the child touching the wall is twisted round so that his arms are crossed. The 'leader' of the line then goes through the arch made by the child touching the wall and his neighbour so that the neighbour twists round as the last child goes through. This is repeated using the first verse only until all the children have crossed arms. The ring then joins up by the first and last child joining crossed hands. During the second verse all shake their heads gravely. For the third verse they slowly squat down and rise again, still holding crossed hands. For the fourth verse they all bend their heads down as low as possible, repeating until the end of the verse.

This is the boat, the golden boat,
   Cup hands together.
That sails on the silver sea,
   Undulate hands like waves.
And these are the oars of ivory white,
   Interlace fingers, palms upwards.
That lift and dip, that lift and dip.
   Lower and raise fingers.
Here are the ten little fairy men
   Show ten fingers up high.
Running along, running along,
   Make fingers 'run'.
To take the oars of ivory white
   Actions as before for last lines.
That lift and dip, that lift and dip,

That move the boat, the golden boat,

Over the silver sea.

A little green frog in a pond am I;
Hoppity, hoppity, hop.
I sit on a little leaf high and dry
And watch all the fishes as they swim by –
Splash! How I make the water fly!
Hoppity, hoppity, hop.

Use the left hand for the leaf and right forefinger for the frog.
Clap hands loudly for the splash.

Two little boats are on the sea,
All is calm as calm can be.
Gently the wind begins to blow,
Two little boats rock to and fro.
Loudly the wind begins to shout,
Two little boats are tossed about.
Gone is the wind, the storm, the rain,
Two little boats sail on again.

Children sit in pairs on the floor facing each other holding hands.
They rock gently or violently as the words indicate and make the following
sound at the end of each line.
1st and 2nd lines: Hum softly.
3rd and 4th lines: OOOOOOOO – OOOOO – OOOOO.
5th and 6th lines: Loud wailing.
7th and 8th lines: Hum softly again.

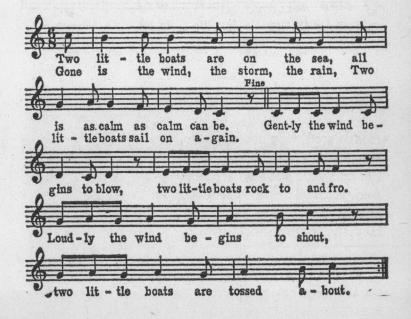

Row, row, row your boat,
Gently down the stream.
Merrily, merrily, merrily, merrily;
Life is but a dream.

*Two children sit facing each other on the floor holding hands,
and sway forwards and backwards.*

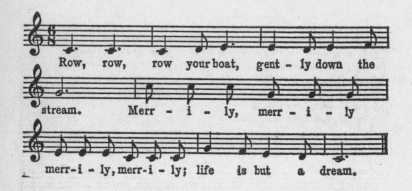

Games to Play with Hands

I can knock with my two hands;
Knock, knock, knock!
I can rock with my two hands;
Rock, rock, rock.
I can tap with my two hands;
Tap, tap, tap!
I can clap with my two hands;
Clap, clap, clap.

Do the actions suggested by the words.

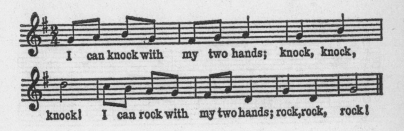

Roly poly, ever so slowly ... ever ... so ... slowly.
Roly poly, faster, faster, FASTER, FASTER!
Roly poly, ever so slowly, etc.

Roll fists round each other as the words suggest.

Fingers like to wiggle, waggle,
Wiggle, waggle, wiggle, waggle,
Fingers like to wiggle, waggle,
Right in front of me.

2nd verse ends: High above my head.

3rd verse ends: Almost on the floor.

4th verse ends: Right out to the sides.

Wiggle fingers as suggested by the words.

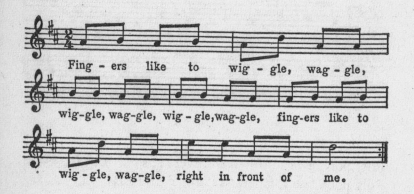

Fing - ers like to wig - gle, wag - gle,
wig-gle, wag-gle, wig - gle, wag-gle, fing-ers like to
wig - gle, wag-gle, right in front of me.

See my fingers walking, walking,
All together in a row.
See my fingers walking, walking,
All together to and fro.
Here is a big house,
Tall and wide.
Knock at the door,
And walk inside!

See my fingers running, etc.

See my fingers jumping, etc.

See my fingers sliding, etc.

Do the actions suggested by the words (make the house by putting two hands together, joined at the finger tips).

Roly poly, roly poly, up, up, up;
    Roll hands round each other moving upwards.
Roly poly, roly poly, down, down, down;
    Roll hands downwards.
Roly poly, roly poly, out, out, out;
    Roll hands away from you.
Roly poly, roly poly, in, in, in;
    Roll hands towards you.

Wind the bobbin up,
Roll fists round each other.
Wind the bobbin up,

Pull, pull, clap, clap, clap;
Pull fists apart as though pulling elastic, then clap.
Point to the ceiling,
Do the actions as they are mentioned.
Point to the floor,

Point to the window,

Point to the door.

Clap your hands together,

One, two, three,

Put your hands upon your knee.

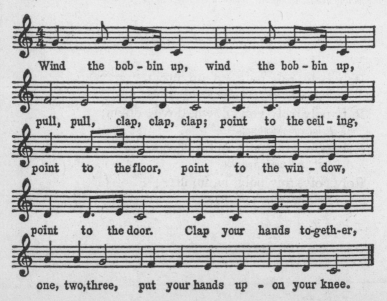

Wind the bob-bin up, wind the bob-bin up,

pull, pull, clap, clap, clap; point to the ceil-ing,

point to the floor, point to the win-dow,

point to the door. Clap your hands to-geth-er,

one, two, three, put your hands up-on your knee.

Let your hands so loudly clap, clap, clap.
Let your fingers loudly snap, snap, snap.
Then fold your arms and shut your eyes,
And quiet be.

Swiftly roll your hands so wide awake.
Let your fingers briskly shake, shake, shake.
Then fold your arms and shut your eyes,
And quiet be.

Let us climb a ladder, do not fall,
Till at last we reach a steeple tall.
Then fold your arms and shut your eyes,
And quiet be.

Do the actions suggested by the words.

You twiddle your thumbs and clap your hands,
And then you stamp your feet.
You turn to the left, you turn to the right,
You make your fingers meet.
You make a bridge, you make an arch,
You give another clap.
You wave your hands, you fold your hands,
Then lay them in your lap.

Do the actions as they are mentioned.

Raise your hands above your head,
Clap them one, two, three;
Rest them now upon your hips,
Slowly bend your knees.
Up again and stand erect,
Put your right foot out;
Shake your fingers, nod your head,
And twist yourself about.

Do the actions suggested by the words.

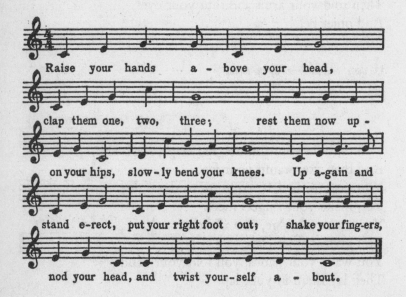

Raise your hands a - bove your head, clap them one, two, three; rest them now up - on your hips, slow - ly bend your knees. Up a-gain and stand e-rect, put your right foot out; shake your fing-ers, nod your head, and twist your-self a - bout.

Ten little gentlemen standing in a row.
Bow, little gentlemen, bow down low;
Walk, little gentlemen, right across the floor,
And don't forget, gentlemen, to please close the door.

Use fingers to represent the gentlemen.
Give a big clap for closing the door.

Heads and shoulders, knees and toes,
Knees and toes, knees and toes,
Heads and shoulders, knees and toes,
We all turn round together.

Touch each part of the body as it is mentioned.

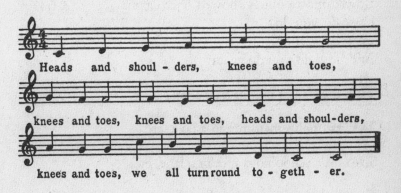

Ten little Indian boys standing in a row,
Hold hands up, fingers straight.

They bow to the Chieftain, very, very low;
Bend all fingers.

They march to the left, then they march to the right;
Move hands to the left wriggling the fingers, then move them to the right.

They all stand up straight, ready to fight.
Straighten all fingers again.

Along came a man with a very big gun –
Hold out two fingers of one hand like a gun.

You should have seen those Indian boys run.
Run fingers along the floor.

This may also be played with children pretending to be the Indians.

Two fat gentlemen met in a lane,
Bowed most politely, bowed once again.
How do you do,
How do you do,
And how do you do again?

Two thin ladies met in a lane, etc.

Two tall policemen met in a lane, etc.

Two little schoolboys met in a lane, etc.

Two little babies met in a lane, etc.

1st verse: Bend thumbs. 2nd verse: Bend forefingers.
3rd verse: Bend middle fingers. 4th verse: Bend ring fingers.
5th verse: Bend little fingers.

Ten little soldiers stand up straight,
Hold up both hands, palms outwards.
Ten little soldiers make a gate,
Reverse hands, hold them downwards.
Ten little soldiers make a ring,
Hold hands with palms facing, little fingers and thumbs touching.
Ten little soldiers bow to the king.
Bend all fingers.
Ten little soldiers dance all day,
Wriggle all fingers.
Ten little soldiers hide away.
Hide fingers behind back.

Number Songs and Rhymes

Five little sparrows sitting in a row;
One said, 'Cheep, cheep, I must go!'
One little, two little,
Three little, four little,
Five little sparrows – Oh.

Four little sparrows sitting in a row, etc.

Three little sparrows sitting in a row, etc.

Two little sparrows sitting in a row, etc.

One little sparrow left in the row
Said, 'Oh, dearie me what shall I do?'
One little, two little,
Three little, four little ...
'Cheep! I'll fly away too.'

Use the fingers of one hand to indicate the number of sparrows.
Repeat the song using the other hand.
Use the tune for 'Ten little nigger boys sitting in a row'.

Five little mice came out to play,
Gathering crumbs up on their way;
Out came a pussy-cat
Sleek and black –
Four little mice went scampering back.

Four little mice came out to play, etc.

Use the fingers on one hand for the mice and the other hand for the cat.

Five little froggies sitting on a well;
One looked up and down he fell;
Froggies jumped high
Froggies jumped low;
Four little froggies dancing to and fro. Etc.

Use fingers to represent frogs, and reduce the number held up for each verse.
Wriggle fingers to represent the actions of the frogs.

Ten fat sausages sitting in the pan;
> *Show ten fingers.*

One went, 'POP!' and another went 'BANG!'
> *Clap hands loudly.*

Eight fat sausages, etc.

Adjust the number of fingers held up in each verse.

Ten galloping horses came through the town.
Five were white and five were brown.
They galloped up and galloped down;
Ten galloping horses came through the town.

Use fingers to represent the horses. 'Gallop' them along the floor and then up
and down.

Five little pussy cats playing near the door;
One ran and hid inside and then there were four.

Four little pussy cats underneath a tree;
One heard a dog bark and then there were three.

Three little pussy cats thinking what to do;
One saw a little bird and then there were two.

Two little pussy cats sitting in the sun;
One ran to catch his tail and then there was one.

One little pussy cat looking for some fun;
He saw a butterfly and then there was none.

Played with the fingers of one hand.

Five little seeds a-sleeping they lay,
A-sleeping they lay.
A bird flew down and took one away –
How many seeds were left that day?

Four little seeds, etc.

Five children curl up on the floor. The child who is the bird stands on a chair with arms outstretched, jumps down and takes one 'seed' away. When all the seeds have been taken the rest of the group blow all the seeds back again.

Five little ladies going for a walk,
Walk fingers of left hand.
Five little ladies stop for a talk.
Tap fingertips together.
Along came five little gentlemen,
Walk fingers of right hand towards others.
They all danced together and that made ten.
Dance all fingers together.

John Brown had a little Indian,
John Brown had a little Indian,
John Brown had a little Indian,
One little Indian boy.

Chorus:
There was one little, two little, three little Indians,
Four little, five little, six little Indians,
Seven little, eight little, nine little Indians,
Ten little Indian boys.

John Brown had two little Indians, etc.

This game can be played with fingers, in which case the last verse is at ten little Indians.
If it is played as a 'bringing in' game it can go on until all the children have been brought into the group.

John Brown had a lit-tle In-dian, John Brown

had a lit-tle In-dian, John Brown

had a lit-tle In-dian, one lit-tle In-dian

Chorus

boy. There was one lit-tle, two lit-tle,

three lit-tle In-dians, four lit-tle, five lit-tle,

six lit-tle In-dians, seven lit-tle, eight lit-tle,

nine lit-tle In-dians, ten lit-tle In-dian boys.

Five little ducks went swimming one day,
Over the pond and far away.
Mother Duck said, 'Quack, quack, quack, quack.'
But only four little ducks came back.

Four little ducks went swimming one day, etc.

Last verse:
One little duck went swimming one day
Over the pond and far away.
Mother Duck says, 'Quack, quack, quack, quack,'
And five little ducks come swimming back.

Use the fingers of one hand and wriggle them to represent the ducks swimming.

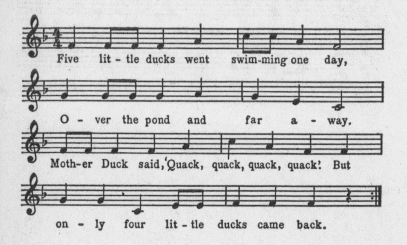

Five lit - tle ducks went swim-ming one day,

O - ver the pond and far a - way.

Moth-er Duck said, 'Quack, quack, quack, quack.' But

on - ly four lit - tle ducks came back.

Games to Play with Feet

Hippety hop to the candy shop
To buy a stick of candy
One for you,
One for me,
One for Sister Sandy.

Use this for a hopping or skipping song.

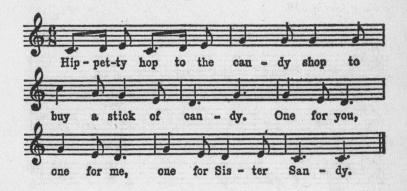

Hip - pet-ty hop to the can - dy shop to
buy a stick of can - dy. One for you,
one for me, one for Sis - ter San - dy.

Can you walk on tip-toe
As softly as a cat?
And can you stamp along the road,
Stamp, stamp, just like that?

Can you take some great big strides
Just like a giant can?
Or walk along so slowly
Like a poor bent old man?

Walk as the words suggest.

We are soldiers marching along,
Left right, left right,
Singing a song;
Hands by side,
Heads quite still,
Down the street and up the hill.

Children march round the room as the words suggest, on the last line lifting knees high as if going up a hill.

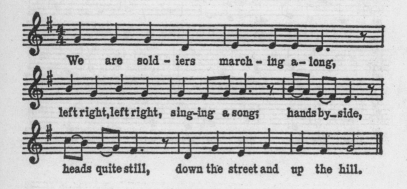

My Wellington boots go thump, thump, thump.
  Stamp feet loudly.
My leather shoes go pit-pat-pit.
  Tread softly.
But my rubber sandals make no noise at all.
  Tread silently.

I can dance upon my toes,
Tra–la–la–la–la.
Softly, softly, on my toes,
Tra–la–la–la–la.
When the dancing tune shall stop,
On the floor I'll gently drop.

Dance as the words suggest, and flop on the floor on the last word.

Up I stretch on tippy toe,
Down to touch my heels I go.
Up again my arms I send,
Down again my knees I bend.

Do the actions suggested by the words.

Up   I   stretch   on   tip - py   toe,
Up   a - gain   my   arms   I   send,

down   to touch   my   heels   I   go.
down   a - gain   my   knees   I   bend.

Stepping over stepping stones, one, two, three,
Stepping over stepping stones, come with me!
The river's very fast,
And the river's very wide,
And we'll step across on stepping stones
And reach the other side.

Children hop across 'stepping stones', improvised from logs, boxes or chalk marks.

Can you walk on two legs, two legs, two legs?
Can you walk on two legs, round and round and round?
I can walk on two legs, two legs, two legs,
I can walk on two legs, round and round and round.

Can you hop on one leg? etc.

Can you wave with one hand? etc.

Can you wave with two hands? etc.

*Do the actions suggested by the words. Children may like to suggest other simple
actions in turn.*

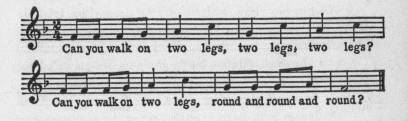

Long legs, long legs, slowly stalking.
> *Take long slow steps.*

Little steps I have to take
> *Take tiny quick steps.*

Because I have such little feet.

See the grown-up people walking.
> *As first line.*

Little ones in little shoes
> *As second line.*

Go pitter-patter down the street.

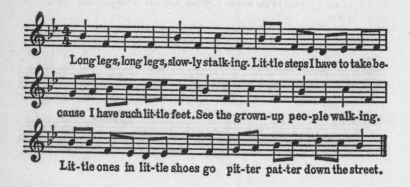

Long legs, long legs, slow-ly stalk-ing. Lit-tle steps I have to take because I have such lit-tle feet. See the grown-up peo-ple walk-ing.
Lit-tle ones in lit-tle shoes go   pit-ter pat-ter down the street.

Moppety-mop and poppety-pop
Went on their way with a skip and a hop;
One with a skip and one with a hop,
Moppety-mop and poppety-pop.

Children skip and hop round the room to the rhythm of the words.

I went to school one morning and I walked like this,
Walked like this, walked like this.
I went to school one morning and I walked like this,
All on my way to school.

I saw a little robin and he hopped like this, etc.

I saw a shiny river and I splashed like this, etc.

I saw a little pony and he galloped like this, etc.

I saw a tall policeman and he stood like this, etc.

I heard the school bell ringing and I ran like this, etc.

Move around the room doing appropriate actions.

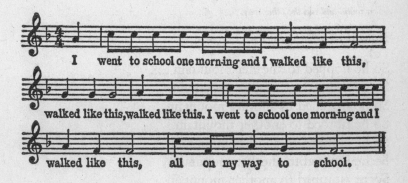

The bear walked over the mountain
The bear walked over the mountain
The bear walked over the mountain
  To see what he could see.

But all that he could see
But all that he could see
Was the other side of the mountain
The other side of the mountain
The other side of the mountain
  Was all that he could see

Children walk round room.

So he ran to another mountain
He ran to another mountain
He ran to another mountain
  To see what he could see

Turn round and run the other way.

But all that he could see ... etc.

So he hopped to another mountain ...
So he skipped to another mountain
So he marched to another mountain
So he tiptoed to another mountain
So he climbed to another mountain
So he jumped to another mountain
So he clumped to another mountain
So he stamped to another mountain

or whatever the children like to suggest for themselves

Sung to the tune of 'For he's a jolly good fellow'

Birds and Animals

This is little Timothy Snail,
Clench right fist with thumb sticking out for head.
His house is on his back.

One day two men came along,

And popped him in a sack.
Right hand covered by left hand.
At last he managed to get out,
Right hand creeps out of left hand.
Out of a hole so small.

What became of him after that
Right hand goes out of sight.
I've never been told at all.
Shake head slowly.

Under a stone where the earth was firm,

I found a wriggly, wriggly worm;
Use one forefinger for the worm and cover i twith the other hand.
'Good morning,' I said.

'How are you today?'
Uncover the forefinger.
But the wriggly worm just wriggled away!
Wriggle the forefinger away up the other arm.

Two little dicky-birds
Use index fingers to represent the birds.
Sitting on a wall,

One named Peter, one named Paul.
Indicate which finger is which bird.
Fly away Peter, fly away Paul;
Put appropriate fingers behind back.
Come back Peter,
Bring each finger back.
Come back Paul.

Two little blackbirds singing in the sun,
One flew away and then there was one;
One little blackbird, very black and small,
He flew away and then there was the wall.
One little brick wall lonely in the rain,
Waiting for the blackbirds to come and sing again.

Use forefingers for the birds. Use folded arms for the wall.

A little brown rabbit popped out of the ground,
Right index finger pops up.

Wriggled his whiskers and looked around.
Right index finger wriggles.

Another wee rabbit who lived in the grass
Left index finger pops up.

Popped his head out and watched him pass.
Right hand hops over left (wrists crossed).

Then both the wee rabbits went hoppity hop,

Hoppity, hoppity, hoppity, hop,
Both index fingers hop forward.

Till they came to a wall and had to stop.
Both fingers stop suddenly.

Then both the wee rabbits turned themselves round,
Hands uncross.

And scuttled off home to their holes in the ground.
Hands hop back and finish in pockets.

Rabbit in a hollow sits and sleeps,
Head sideways on folded hands.

Hunter in the forest nearer creeps.
Hand movement to indicate creeping.

Little rabbit sitting there,

Have a care.
Hands up to head to make rabbit ears.

Quickly, little rabbit,

You must run, run, RUN!
Hands indicate running.

A mouse lived in a little hole,
One hand curled inside the other.
Lived softly in a little hole.

When all was quiet as quiet can be (Sh! Sh!),

When all was quiet as quiet can be (Sh! Sh!),
Said very softly.
Out popped HE!
Right hand jumps out of left.

Creep, little mousie, come along to me,
Creep fingers along the floor.
Creep, little mousie, I've a cake for tea.

Puss, Puss, Puss, Puss, where is little mouse?
Walk along the floor on all fours looking everywhere.
Safe, safe, safe, safe, in his little house!
*Sit on the floor again, one fist lightly clenched to make
a 'house' for the index finger.*

One, two, three, four, One, two, three, four,

These little pussy cats came to my door.
Hold up the four fingers of right hand and count them.
They just stood there and said 'Good day,'
Make the fingers bow on 'Good day'.
And then they tiptoed right away.
*Walk the fingers away over the front of the body and
behind the left shoulder.*

If I were a little bird, high up in the sky,
This is how I'd flap my wings and fly, fly, fly.

If I were a friendly dog, going for a run,
This is how I'd wag my tail when having fun.

If I were a cat I'd sit by the fireplace,
This is how I'd use my paws to wash my face.

If I were a rabbit small, in the woods I'd roam,
This is how I'd dig a burrow for my home.

If I were an elephant, very big and strong,
This is how I'd wave my trunk and walk along.

If I were a kangaroo, I would leap and bound,
This is how I'd jump about and hop around.

If I were a camel tall, slowly I would stride,
This is how I'd rock and sway from side to side.

If I were a tall giraffe, living in the Zoo,
This is how I'd bend my neck and look at you.

Mime the actions suggested by the words.

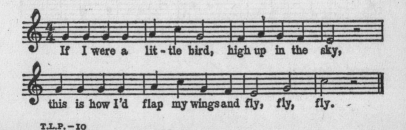

If I were a lit-tle bird, high up in the sky, this is how I'd flap my wings and fly, fly, fly.

T.L.P.—10

See the little bunny sleeping,
Till it's nearly noon.
Come and let us gently wake him
With a merry tune.
Oh, how still!
Is he ill?
Wake up soon.

Hop, little bunny, hop, hop, hop.
Hop, little bunny, hop, hop, hop.

Children pretend to be sleeping rabbits.
Clap loudly after 'Wake up soon'.
Children then hop round the room.

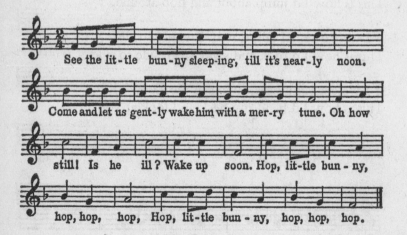

I have made a pretty nest,
Interlock fingers, palms upwards.
Look inside, look inside.

Hungry birdies with their beaks
*Place index fingers and thumbs of each hand together
and 'open and close' them.*
Open wide, open wide.

See my little birdies grow,
Gradually spread hands apart to indicate growth.
Day by day, day by day,

Till they spread their little wings,
Cross arms at the wrist and flap hands.
And then they fly away.

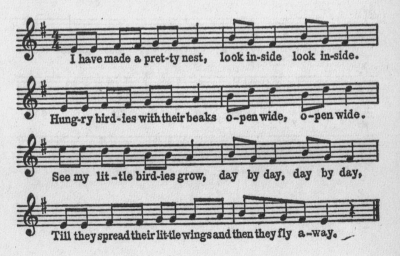

Incy Wincy Spider climbed up the water spout,
Use the fingers of both hands to represent a spider climbing up.

Down came the rain drops and washed poor Incy out;
Raise the hands and lower them slowly, wriggling fingers to indicate rain.

Out came the sunshine and dried up all the rain,
Raise hands above the head together and bring them out and down.

And Incy Wincy Spider climbed up that spout again.
As first line.

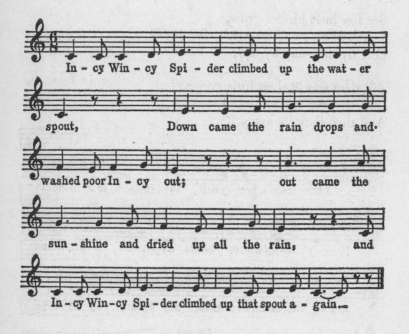

My pigeon house I open wide
And I set all my pigeons free.
They fly around on every side
And perch on the highest tree.
And when they return
From their merry flight,
They close their eyes
And say, 'Good night.'
Coo-oo Coo, Coo-oo Coo,
Coo-oo Coo, Coo-oo Coo,
Coo-oo Coo, Coo-oo Coo, Coo-oo.

This may be played as a game with a ring of children as the pigeon house with two or three acting as the pigeons, or by each child miming the actions suggested by the words.

Pretty little pussy cat,
Sitting there upon the mat,
Show me how you arch your back,
Pretty little pussy cat.

Children go round the room on all fours and on the last line arch their backs.

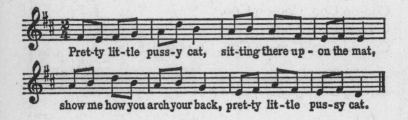

Pret-ty lit-tle puss-y cat, sit-ting there up - on the mat,

show me how you arch your back, pret-ty lit-tle pus-sy cat.

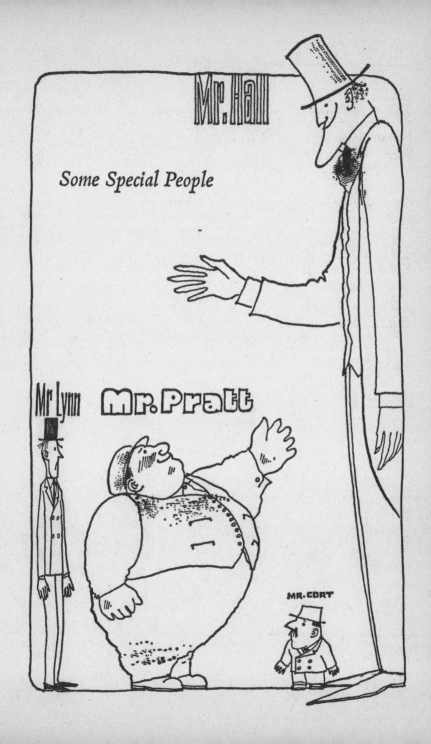

Some Special People

The policeman walks with heavy tread,
Left, right, left, right.
Swings his arms, holds up his head,
Left, right, left, right.

Mime as the words suggest.

There's a cobbler down our street
Mending shoes for little feet.
With a bang and a bang and a bang, bang, bang;
And a bang and a bang and a bang, bang, bang!

Mending shoes the whole day long,
Mending shoes to make them strong,
With a bang, etc.

1st verse: Hammer fist on fist.
2nd verse: Hammer with feet.

Old John Muddlecombe lost his cap,
    Put hands on head.
He couldn't find it anywhere, the poor old chap.
    Pretend to look for hat.
He walked down the High Street, and everybody said,
    Walk slowly round the room.
'Silly John Muddlecombe, you've got it on your HEAD!'
    Shake finger at imaginary old man.
    Then put hands on head.

One morning the little Indian boy woke up,
Put one finger up behind head to represent a feather. Stretch and yawn.
Got out of bed,

And said to his mummy,

'Oooooooh, ooooh –
Waggle one finger in the mouth to make an Indian call.
I'm going for a walk.'

He went down the garden path and shut the gate –
Slap knees.
SLAM!

He went down the road till he came to a bridge.
Clap hands.
He walked across the bridge –

Trip, trap –

And he walked along the road till he came to a river.
Slap chest.
He looked up the river and down the river.
Look left and right.
There was no bridge so he swam –
Make swimming actions.
Splish, splash.

When he got to the other side he walked in the forest till
    he came to a great big tree.
Slap knees.
He looked round this side of the tree,
Look left and right.
And he looked round that side of the tree,

But there was nothing there.

Then he heard a noise –

Tigers!

He ran through the forest –
     Reverse all actions as fast as possible.
He swam across the river –

He ran across the bridge –

He shut the gate . . . SLAM –

He ran in to his mother –

'Oooooh, ooooh,' he said,

'I'm home.'

See the soldiers in the street,
Hear the marching of their feet;
They are singing as they go,
Marching, marching, to and fro:
See the soldiers in the street,
Hear the marching of their feet.

Children march round separately or in a long file.
Use the tune of 'Twinkle, twinkle little star'.

Now I'll tell you a story, and this story is new,

So you listen carefully, and do as I do.

This is Tom Thumb – and this is his house;
Hold up thumb, then make a roof shape with two forefingers.
These are his windows, and this is Squeaky, his mouse.
Make 'spectacles', then hold up one finger for the mouse.
One morning very early the sun began to shine;
Indicate the sunshine with arms held high, then gradually lowered.
Squeaky mouse sat up in bed and counted up to nine.
Wriggle the 'mouse' finger and point to nine fingers in turn.
Then Squeaky made a jump – right on to Tom Thumb's
bed;
Jump the 'mouse' finger on to the other hand.
She quickly ran right up his arm and sat upon his head.
Run the finger right up the arm and on to the head.
Squeaky pulled his hair, and Squeaky pulled his nose,
Pretend to pull hair and nose.
Until Tom Thumb jumped out of bed

And put on all his clothes.
Run thumb and forefinger down the 'Tom' thumb to indicate dressing.
Then they sat down to breakfast
Mime the actions.
And ate some crusty bread,

And when that was all quite finished

Little Tom Thumb said,

'Now I'll tell you a story, and this story is new . . .' etc.

Little Arabella Miller
Found a woolly caterpillar.
First it crawled upon her mother,
Then upon her baby brother;
All said, 'Arabella Miller,
Take away that caterpillar.'

Pretend to pick up the caterpillar; walk fingers of right hand up the left arm then vice versa; pretend to put the caterpillar down.

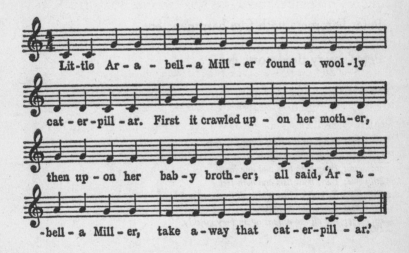

Peter hammers with one hammer,
One hammer, one hammer,
Peter hammers with one hammer,
All day long.

Peter hammers with two hammers, etc.

Peter hammers with three hammers, etc.

Peter hammers with four hammers, etc.

Peter hammers with five hammers, etc.

Peter's very tired now, etc.

Peter's wide awake now, etc.

1st verse: Bang on the floor with one foot.
2nd verse: Bang with two fists.
3rd verse: Bang both fists and one foot.
4th verse: Bang both fists and both feet.
5th verse: Bang both fists and both feet, and nod head.
6th verse: Rest head on hands.
7th verse: Do all the actions again very quickly.

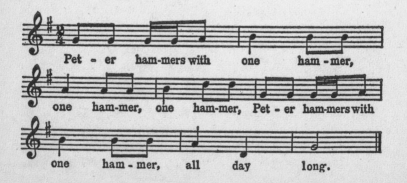

Willum he had seven sons,
Seven sons, seven sons;
Willum he had seven sons,
And this is what they did.

Children take it in turns to suggest an action to be mimed, e.g. chopping wood, drawing water, milking cows. The music is repeated to accompany the actions.

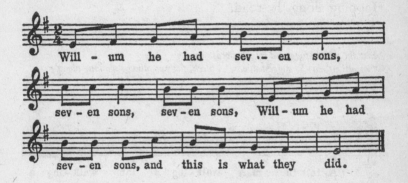

Will - um   he   had   sev - en   sons,
sev - en sons,   sev - en sons,   Will - um   he   had
sev - en   sons, and   this   is   what   they   did.

Mr Lynn is very thin,
  Palms close together.

Mr Pratt is very fat,
  Hands cupped together.

Mr Cort is very short,
  Hands near the ground.

Mr Hall is very tall,
  Hands stretched up high.

Mr Dent is very bent,
  Hands bent in half.

Mr Wait is very straight.
  Hands stiffly upright.

A tall thin man walking along,
Walking along, walking along!
A tall thin man walking along,
Walking along the road.

A fat little frog hopping along,
Hopping along, hopping along;
A fat little frog hopping along,
Hopping along the road.

Mime the actions suggested by the words.
Other actions may be suggested, e.g. 'A black, floppy golliwog walking along';
'A stiff wooden dolly walking along'.

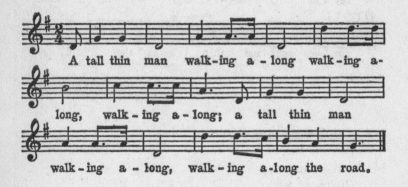

A tall thin man walk-ing a - long walk-ing a-
long, walk-ing a - long; a tall thin man
walk-ing a - long, walk-ing a-long the road.

Tommy Thumb, Tommy Thumb,
Where are you?
Here I am, here I am,
How do you do?

Peter Pointer, Peter Pointer, etc.

Toby Tall, Toby Tall, etc.

Ruby Ring, Ruby Ring, etc.

Baby Small, Baby Small, etc.

Fingers All, Fingers All, etc.

Bring hands out from behind back after 'Where are you?'
1st verse: Wriggle both thumbs and make them bow on the last line.
2nd verse: Repeat, using index fingers.
3rd verse: Use middle fingers.
4th verse: Use ring fingers.
5th verse: Use little fingers.
6th verse: Use all fingers.

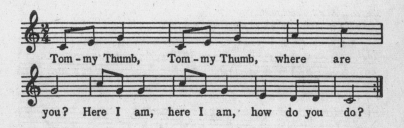

Last evening Cousin Peter came,
Last evening Cousin Peter came,
Last evening Cousin Peter came,
To say that he was here.

He hung his hat upon a peg,
He hung his hat upon a peg,
He hung his hat upon a peg,
To show that he was here.

He wiped his shoes upon the mat, etc.

He kicked his shoes off one by one, etc.

He danced about in his stockinged feet, etc.

He played he was a great big bear, etc.

He tossed us up into the air, etc.

He made a bow and said 'Good-bye', etc.

1st verse: March round room.
Other verses: Mime the actions suggested by the words.

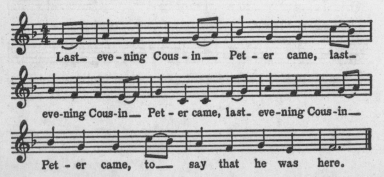

Mr Jumping Jack Man is a funny, funny man;
Plain jumping for first two lines.

He jumps and jumps as fast as he can;

His arms go out and his legs go too;
Appropriate movements.

Mr Jumping Jack Man, how do you do?
Bow twice (on each 'do').

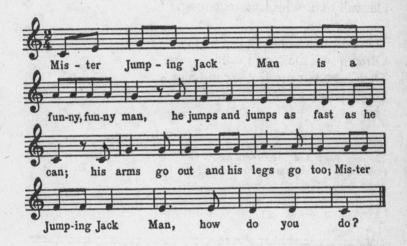

Slowly, slowly walks my Granddad,
Leaning hard upon his stick.
'Wait for me, my lad,' says Granddad,
'I'm too old, I can't be quick.'

Father goes to work each morning,
This is how he walks along.
He is not so old as Granddad,
He walks fast – his legs are strong.

When to school I have to hurry,
Often down the road I run.
Then how fast my feet are moving –
Like a race – I think it's fun.

Walk round the room as the words suggest.
The same tune is used for each verse but the time is altered
from slow to very quick to suit the words.

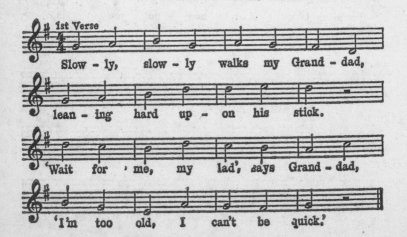

173

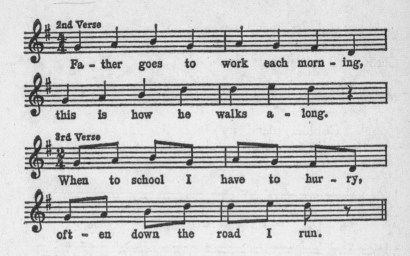

Chip-chop, chip-chop, Chipper, Chopper Joe,
Chip-chop, chip-chop, Chipper, Chopper Joe.
One big blow!
Ouch! my toe!
Chipper Chopper Joe chops wood just so!

Children pretend to chop down trees, hop on one foot on the fourth line, then chop again on the last ine.

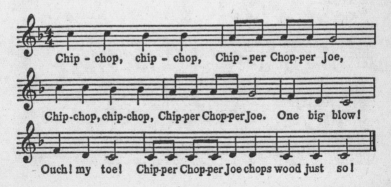

Cobbler, Cobbler, mend my shoe,
Hammer with fists on knees.
Get it done by half past two.

My toe is peeping through,
Drum feet on floor.
Cobbler, Cobbler, mend my shoe.
Hammer with fists on knees.

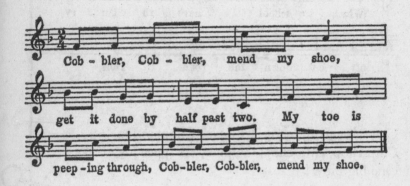

Singing and Dancing Games

Look who comes here, Punchinello little fellow,
Look who comes here, Punchinello little man.

What can you do, Punchinello little fellow?
What can you do, Punchinello little man?

We'll do it too, Punchinello little fellow,
We'll do it too, Punchinello little man!

The children stand in a ring while the one chosen to be Punchinello skips round inside. During the second verse he performs some action. During the third verse the children copy him.

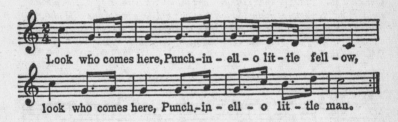

Look who comes here, Punch-in-ell-o lit-tle fell-ow,
look who comes here, Punch-in-ell-o lit-tle man.

Can you tell me what the boys do,
Can you tell me what they do?
All the boys are (dancing),
And (Johnny) can dance too.

(Johnny) can (dance) in a great big ring,
A great big ring,
A great big ring,
(Johnny) can (dance) in a great big ring,
Like all the other boys.

*One child or an adult sings the first verse and the other children suggest some action,
e.g. hopping, skipping, marching, in the third line and the name of one child in the
group in the fourth line. For the second verse the chosen child does the chosen action
all round the ring, while the others sing the second verse to the tune of the
'Mulberry Bush'.*

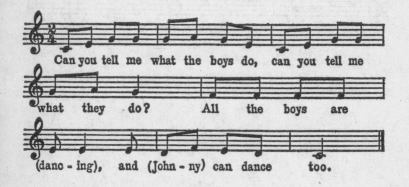

Can you tell me what the boys do, can you tell me
what they do? All the boys are
(danc - ing), and (John - ny) can dance too.

What shall we do when we all go out,
All go out, all go out,
What shall we do when we all go out,
All go out to play?

We shall play with a skipping rope, etc.

We shall play with a whip and top, etc.

We shall ride our tricycles, etc.

Children can suggest different items and suitable actions.

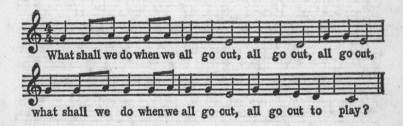

What shall we do when we all go out, all go out, all go out,

what shall we do when we all go out, all go out to play?

Did you ever see a lassie (laddie),
A lassie, a lassie,
Did you ever see a lassie
Go this way and that?

Go this way and that way,
And this way and that way.
Did you ever see a lassie
Go this way and that?

During the first verse one child dances alone in the ring making some distinctive action. During the second verse all the others imitate what he did. Another child then goes into the middle to be the lassie or the laddie.

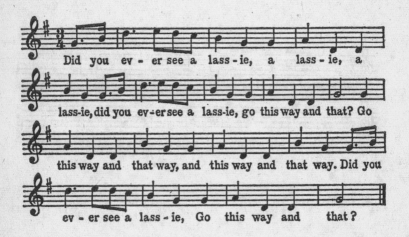

Did you ev-er see a lass-ie, a lass-ie, a
lass-ie, did you ev-er see a lass-ie, go this way and that? Go
this way and that way, and this way and that way. Did you
ev-er see a lass-ie, Go this way and that?

We all clap hands together,
We all clap hands together,
We all clap hands together,
As children like to do.

Other verses:
We all stand up together, etc.

We all sit down together, etc.

We all stamp feet together, etc.

We all turn round together, etc.

*Children like to make suggestions of their own, and the words
may have to be fitted in quickly on one note.*

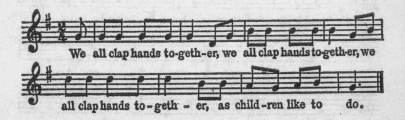

As I was walking down the street,
Heigh-ho, heigh-ho, heigh-ho,
A little friend I chanced to meet,
Heigh-ho, heigh-ho, heigh-ho!
Jiggety jig and away we go,
Away we go, away we go,
Jiggety jig and away we go,
Heigh-ho, heigh-ho, heigh-ho!

Children skip round the room alone, then join hands
with a friend and skip holding hands.

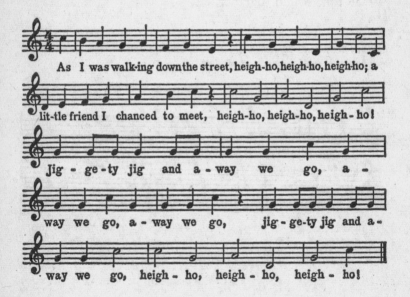

Slip one and two,
>   *Children join hands in a circle and take two sliding steps to the left.*

Jump three and four,
>   *Make two little jumps. Drop hands.*

Turn around swiftly
>   *Turn round once.*

And sit upon the floor.
>   *Sit on the floor with legs crossed.*

Clap one and two,
>   *Clap twice.*

Nod three and four,
>   *Nod twice.*

Jump up again
>   *Jump up.*

And be ready for more.
>   *Join hands again ready for the next time.*

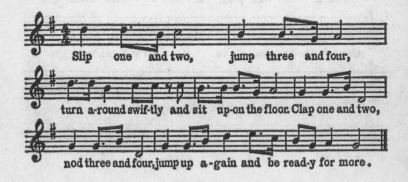

Oh, we can play on the big bass drum,
And this is the music to it;
Boom, boom, boom goes the big bass drum,
And that's the way we do it.

Oh, we can play on the triangle, etc.
(Tang, tang, tang)

Oh, we can play on the castanets, etc.
(Clack, clack, clack)

*The children sit down on the floor and pretend to play each instrument as it is
included. They will suggest many more. On the last time it is sung they can each
choose an instrument for themselves and make all the different noises at the same
time.*

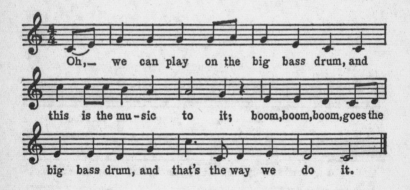

Old Roger is dead and he lies in his grave,
Lies in his grave, lies in his grave.
Old Roger is dead and he lies in his grave,
Heigh ho, lies in his grave.

Other verses:
They planted an apple tree over his head, etc.

The apples grew ripe and they all tumbled down, etc.

There came an old woman a-picking them up, etc.

Old Roger got up and he gave her a poke, etc.

This made the old woman go hippety-hop, etc.

One child lies in the centre of the ring of children who walk round as they sing.
For apple trees, raise arms above the head.
For apples tumbling, drop fingers with a wriggling movement.
One child then pretends to pick up the apples and put them in her apron.
Roger gets up and pokes her.
The old woman hops all round the ring.

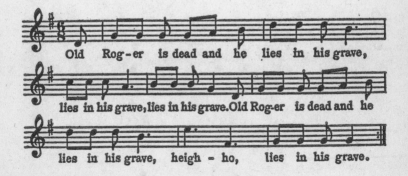

There's a little ball, such a tiny little ball,
Which we hope you cannot see.
There's a little ball, such a weeny, woolly ball;
Can you guess in whose hand it will be?

*One child hides his eyes in the middle of the ring and at the end of
the verse he opens his eyes and tries to guess who is holding the ball.*

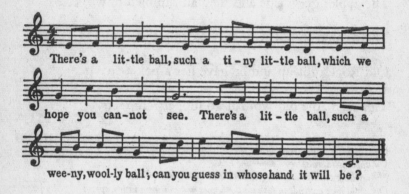

There's a lit-tle ball, such a ti-ny lit-tle ball, which we
hope you can-not see. There's a lit-tle ball, such a
wee-ny, wool-ly ball; can you guess in whose hand it will be?

Sometimes I'm very, very small,
Sometimes I'm very, very tall:
Shut your eyes and turn around
And guess which I am now.

This may be played with two or more children. One child covers his eyes while the others sing and has to guess whether they are standing tall or crouching down at the end of the song. If he guesses right he has another turn.

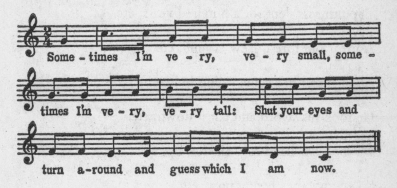

Some - times I'm ve - ry, ve - ry small, some -
times I'm ve - ry, ve - ry tall: Shut your eyes and
turn a-round and guess which I am now.

There was a princess long ago,
Long ago, long ago,
There was a princess long ago,
Long ago.

And she lived in a big high tower, etc.

One day a fairy waved her wand, etc.

The princess slept for a hundred years, etc.

A great big forest grew around, etc.

A gallant prince came riding by, etc.

He took his sword and cut it down, etc.

He took her hand to wake her up, etc.

So everybody's happy now, etc.

1st verse: The 'princess' stands in the centre of the ring of children.
2nd verse: The children raise their joined hands to make the tower.
3rd verse: One child chosen as the fairy waves her arm over the princess.
4th verse: The princess lies down and closes her eyes.
5th verse: The children wave their arms as trees.
6th verse: One child chosen as the prince gallops round the outside of the ring.
7th verse: He pretends to cut down the trees.
8th verse: He wakes up the princess.
9th verse: Children skip round clapping their hands.

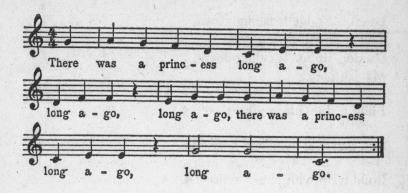

There was a princ-ess long a-go,
long a-go, long a-go, there was a princ-ess
long a-go, long a-go.

Round and round the village,
Round and round the village,
Round and round the village,
As we have done before.

In and out the windows, etc.

Take yourself a partner, etc.

Bow (curtsey) before you leave her (him), etc.

1st verse: One child skips round outside the ring of children.
2nd verse: He then skips in and out under their raised arms.
3rd verse: He takes a partner and dances with her in the ring.
4th verse: He bows to her then rejoins the ring. She then repeats the game.
Use the traditional tune.

London Bridge is falling down,
Falling down, falling down,
London Bridge is falling down,
My fair lady.

Build it up with iron bars, etc.

Iron bars will bend and bow, etc.

Build it up with pins and needles, etc.

Pins and needles will rust and bend, etc.

Build it up with penny loaves, etc.

Penny loaves will tumble down, etc.

Build it up with gold and silver, etc.

Gold and silver I've not got, etc.

Here's a prisoner I have got, etc.

What's the prisoner done to you? etc.

Stole my watch and broke my chain, etc.

What'll you take to set him free, etc.

One hundred pounds will set him free, etc.

One hundred pounds we have not got, etc.

Then off to prison he must go, etc.

Two children hold hands high to form the bridge and agree secretly which is to be
'gold' and which 'silver'. The other children file through the bridge and one is
caught each time on the word 'lady'. He must choose in a whisper whether he is
to be gold or silver and goes behind the appropriate side of the bridge. The bridge
children and the file sing alternate verses of the song, the file starting with the
first verse. When all the children have been caught there is a tug of war.
This would be much too long for very small children. It can be finished after 'Gold
and silver I've not got' by the file singing 'We will be your gold and silver'. Each
child chooses secretly which to be.
Use the traditional tune.

Here we go gathering nuts in May,
Nuts in May, nuts in May,
Here we go gathering nuts in May,
On a cold and frosty morning.

Who will you have for nuts in May, etc.

We'll have — for nuts in May, etc.

Who will you send to fetch her away, etc.

We'll send — to fetch her away, etc.

The children are divided to form two lines. During the first verse the two lines
advance and retreat facing each other. During the second verse one line only advances
and retreats. For verse three the other side advances and retreats, choosing the name
of one of the opposite side. For verse four the first side again come up and ask,
'Who will you send to fetch her away?' In verse five the other side choose the
name of one of their own team. The two children chosen have a tug of war until one
child is pulled to the other side and is then a member of that team. This could go on
for a long time and it may be a good idea to say how many times it will be repeated
before the winning team is judged.
Use the traditional tune.

A-hunting we will go,
A-hunting we will go;
We'll catch a fox
And put him in a box,
And never let him go.

Partners stand facing each other and almost touching their neighbour to form a wide lane. The first couple hold hands and skip sideways down to the end of the lane and back. Once back at the top they loose hands and skip round the back of the line they stand in. The other children follow. At the bottom of the line the leaders meet their partners once more and make an arch, and the other children go through it in pairs. The first couple now stay at the bottom of the line, and the pair who are now at the top repeat the whole sequence. The game goes on until all the children have had a turn, and the first pair are back at the top.
Use the traditional tune.

Oh, the grand old Duke of York,
He had ten thousand men.
He marched them up to the top of the hill
And he marched them down again.

Chorus:
And when they were up they were up,
And when they were down they were down;
And when they were only half-way up
They were neither up nor down.

Oh, the grand old Duke of York,
He had ten thousand men.
They beat their drums to the top of the hill
And they beat them down again.

Other verses:
They played their pipes to the top of the hill.

They banged their guns to the top of the hill.

*Children march in line across the room and back doing the appropriate actions.
Use the traditional tune.*

Here we go Looby Loo,
Here we go Looby Light,
Here we go Looby Loo,
All on a Saturday night.

You put your right foot in,
You put your right foot out,
You shake it a little, a little,
And turn yourself about.

You put your left foot in, etc.

You put your right hand in, etc.

You put your left hand in, etc.

You put your whole self in, etc.

*During the first verse the children skip round in a ring.
In the following verses they do the appropriate actions.
Use the traditional tune.*

O do you know the Muffin Man,
The Muffin Man, the Muffin Man,
O do you know the Muffin Man,
Who lives in Drury Lane?

O yes, I know the Muffin Man,
The Muffin Man, the Muffin Man,
O yes, I know the Muffin Man,
Who lives in Drury Lane.

*One child is blindfolded and holds a stick (or rolled newspaper) in the middle of the ring. During the first verse the ring walks round the blindfolded one. At the end of the first verse the one in the middle touches someone in the ring, who must then hold the other end of the stick. This child sings the second verse and if the blindfolded child can guess who it is they change places. If he does not guess correctly he has to stay blindfolded while the verse is sung again and he touches someone else.
Use the traditional tune.*

I sent a letter to my love
And on the way I dropped it;
One of you has picked it up
And put it in your pocket.

*All the children except one sit down in a ring. The odd one runs round the outside of the ring while the song is sung and drops a handkerchief behind one of the seated children. At the end of the verse both the odd child and the one who had the 'letter' dropped behind him run round the ring in opposite directions and try to sit down in the empty space. The one who loses the race has to be the odd one for the next time.
Use the traditional tune.*

Poor Jenny sits a-weeping,
A-weeping, a-weeping,
Poor Jenny sits a-weeping,
On a bright summer's day.

Oh, why is she weeping, etc.

She's weeping for a sweetheart, etc.

Now Jenny choose a sweetheart, etc.

Now Jenny choose your bridesmaids, etc.

Now Jenny choose a page-boy, etc.

Now Jenny choose the parson, etc.

Now Jenny shall be married, etc.

1st, 2nd, 3rd verses: The child chosen to be Jenny sits in the middle of the ring while the others dance round her, changing direction at the end of each verse.
4th, 5th, 6th, 7th verses: At the end of each of these verses Jenny chooses a child, or two where relevant, to join her in the ring.
8th verse: All the children form a procession led by the parson, followed by Jenny and her retinue.
Use the traditional tune.

She'll be coming round the mountain when she comes,
Toot, Toot!
She'll be coming round the mountain when she comes,
Toot, Toot!
She'll be coming round the mountain –
She'll be coming round the mountain –
She'll be coming round the mountain when she comes,
Toot, Toot!

She'll be riding six white horses when she comes, Whoa
back, etc.
(*On last line add:* Toot, Toot!)

And we'll all go out to meet her when she comes, Hi babe,
etc.
(*On last line add:* Whoa back, Toot, Toot!)

And we'll kill the old red rooster when she comes, Chop,
chop! etc.
(*On last line add:* Hi babe, Whoa back, Toot, Toot!)

And we'll all have chicken and dumplings when she comes,
Yum, yum! etc.

(*On last line add:* Chop, chop, Hi babe, Whoa back, Toot,
Toot!)

Actions:
Toot, toot   – *pretend to pull the whistle-cord.*
Whoa back – *pretend to pull on the reins.*
Hi babe   – *wave vigorously.*
Chop, chop – *pretend to hold a chicken with one hand and chop at its
                neck with the other.*
Yum, yum – *rub tummy.*
Use the traditional tune.

'Oranges and lemons,'
Say the bells of Saint Clement's.
'You owe me five farthings,'
Say the bells of Saint Martin's.
'When will you pay me?'
Say the bells of Old Bailey.
'When I grow rich,'
Say the bells of Shoreditch.
'Pray when will that be?'
Say the bells of Stepney.
'I'm sure I don't know,'
Says the great bell of Bow.*
'Brickbats and tiles,'
Say the bells of Saint Giles'.
'Old Father Baldpate,'
Say the slow bells at Aldgate.
'Pokers and tongs,'
Say the bells of Saint John's.
'Kettles and pans,'
Say the bells of Saint Anne's.
'Pancakes and fritters,'
Say the bells of Saint Peter's.
'Two sticks and an apple,'
Say the bells of Whitechapel.
Here comes the candle to light you to bed.
And here comes the chopper to chop off your HEAD.

An arch is formed by two children, who agree secretly which is to be oranges and which lemons. All the other children file under the arch. On 'Here comes the candle' the children forming the arch bring their arms down on each child going through and release him again except for the one caught on 'HEAD'. He has to choose in a whisper whether he wants to be an orange or a lemon and then goes behind the appropriate side of the arch. When all the children are behind the arch on one side or the other there is a tug of war.
Small children would find ending the verse at * easier and quicker.
Use the traditional tune.

On the bridge at Avignon,
They are dancing, they are dancing,
On the bridge at Avignon,
They are dancing in a ring:

Chorus:
The gentlemen go this way,
    (Bow very low)
And then again go this way.

The ladies they go this way, etc.
    (Curtsey)

The nursemaids they go this way, etc.
    (Rock the baby)

The soldiers they go this way, etc.
    (Salute smartly)

All the children dance round in a ring during the verse. During the chorus they do the appropriate action at the end of each line. Many more people will be suggested by the children. Usually the verse is repeated after each chorus but this might be too long for very small children.
Use the traditional tune.

There was a jolly miller and he lived by himself,
As the wheel went round he made his wealth;
With one hand on the hopper and the other on the bag,
As the wheel went round he made his grab.

Boys form an outer ring, girls an inner ring, and they march or skip in opposite directions. The 'miller' stands in the centre. On the word 'grab', each boy grabs a partner from the girls' ring, and the miller does the same. The odd boy out is the next miller.
Use the traditional tune.

Index of First Lines

Some other useful Young Puffin Originals for mothers
with young children

The Puffin Book of Nursery Rhymes

Iona and Peter Opie

Here is a notable collection of nursery rhymes, for it is a fresh gathering from the memories of grandmothers and the byways of folk literature. As well as containing all the familiar jingles it introduces a number of traditional rhymes which have hitherto been known only locally or in individual families. In fact, this is a sparkling treasury of memorable verses, as lovingly planned as a poetry anthology. To complete the pleasure, the book is illustrated on almost every page with exquisite pictures by Pauline Baynes.

All The Year Round

Toni Arthur

Startling secrets, amazing anecdotes, handy hints – they're all in this fascinating book which is packed full of things to make and do, traditional customs and stories, songs and games to keep children occupied and interested during the dullest times of the year. Children of all ages will love this book and parents will find it a boon.

The Young Puffin Book of Verse

compiled by Barbara Ireson

This is a collection of poems, verses, nursery rhymes and jingles for children up to the age of eight. It is an introduction to a vast heritage of poetry. Though diverse in form, language, mood and subject, each poem has been chosen with care as being within the grasp of young readers and listeners.

There are poems included by writers whose names are bywords in the world of children's literature: Edward Lear, Kate Greenaway and Walter de la Mare, as well as many poems by writers whose names are normally found only in collections for adults: Robert Frost, W. B. Yeats, James Kirkup. All the poets with whom modern children are familiar are here too, including James Reeves, Rachel Field, Eleanor Farjeon and Leonard Clark. Finally, there are also many anonymous poems.

Something to Make

Felicia Law

What can you make with yoghourt pots, bits of shiny paper, scraps of fabric, cotton reels, tinsel string, old Christmas cards, odd bits of wool and ribbon, cardboard rolls, egg boxes, and that kind of stuff?

All sorts of things. Collages for instance, and peg dolls and weather charts, scrap books, potato cuts, a snake to keep out the draughts, a purse with your initials on it, a papier mâché owl, paper flowers, a Christmas stable, a wall plaque, cotton-reel animals, a woolly ball for a baby, a tie-and-dye handkerchief and a melon-seed necklace.

This is a wonderfully varied and practical collection of things for children to make from the odds and ends around the home, with very little extra outlay of money. The author has taught art and handicrafts, and knows from experience exactly what children can tackle most successfully.

For parents to work with children up to seven, and then for children to discover for themselves.